WENDIGO

John Bushore

John Bushore

Wendigo © 2013 by John Bushore

This book is a work of fiction. Characters, places, and incidents are the product of the author's imagination or are used fictitiously. Any resemblance to any actual persons, living or dead, events or locales is entirely coincidental.

A MonkeyJohn Books Production

First Edition: April 2013

To order additional copies of this book, visit the author's website at:
http://www.johnbushore.com

ISBN-13:
978-0615794310 (MonkeyJohn Books)

ISBN-10:
0615794319

WENDIGO

CONTENTS

John Bushore

Other books by John Bushore

Wolfwraith (Shadow Fletcher Mystery)
Friends in Dark Places
The Prisoners of Gender
Boy in Chains
"…and Remember that I Am a Man."
Necessary Evil
Going Native (horror anthology)
What's Under the Bed (children's book)

PROLOGUE

I just love this park, Caitlin thought. It was one of the prettiest that she and her family had ever visited, even though it was a bit scary with all the cliffs along the trail. And, if only her little sister, Emily, would ever shut up, Caitlin might see a bird or a squirrel or something. One of the rangers back at the campground had said there were golden eagles in the park.

The park had just opened for the season a couple of weeks ago, she had been told. Just in time for her parents to bring them up here for Spring Break. There had been the added treat of waking up in the campground this morning with a light blanket of snow outside the RV. That was because they were so high in the mountains, she supposed. Tulips and daffodils were already up, back at home, and the trees were beginning to sprout leaves.

The day was warming now and most of the snow had melted, but there were still patches in the shade. She glanced back to where Mom and Dad were following along the river, with Emily wailing something about a stone in her shoe. They stopped and Dad bent over to look at her foot. Good! Maybe Caitlin could get a little farther away while they were stopped.

The trail turned left and she followed it around. Suddenly it was like she was the only person in the whole world. They hadn't seen anyone on the trail at all, but she'd still been with her family. Now it was just her.

This was great! It was like being in the Pocahontas movie she watched all the time. She loved being in the mountains alone on such a beautiful day. The waters of a small creek, below her on the right, tumbled over and around the rocks with a burbling sound, and the soft wind caused a gentle rustle in the trees, which were still bare. Somewhere ahead, a bird—she couldn't tell what kind—trilled, and she became aware she could no longer hear her little sister's voice, only the sounds of the mountains.

She hurried ahead, glad for this chance to stretch her legs after being cooped up in the RV with Emily for the last day and night. No matter what DVD Caitlin wanted to watch, her little sister always insisted on something else. And Mom always sided with Emily, just to shut her up.

A crackle sounded in the dry leaves nearby and Caitlin had the creepy feeling of being watched. She slowed and was about to turn back to rejoin her parents when, suddenly, almost on top of her, she heard something coming toward her from the woods with a loud commotion. She whirled, expecting to spy a bear or some other animal coming down the slope at her.

Instead, two chattering squirrels chased after each other through the sticks and leaves on the ground. They didn't even seem to notice her as they passed within ten feet and then spiraled up a tree trunk like out-of-control cartoon creatures.

Her head went back, her eyes following them into the treetops. Wouldn't it be neat if she could find their nest and see baby squirrels? But sunlight glinted in her eyes and she soon lost sight of them, her vision momentarily hazy.

A loud, whistling call came from the river and she turned to look. There was some kind of duck waddling along the rocks of the opposite creek bank. And behind it, coming out of the bushes was a mama duck, followed by a half-a-dozen little yellow and brown fuzz balls with scurrying orange feet. Babies! She rushed ahead, past a large, overhanging rock and stopped where she could look down upon them more closely.

As she watched the family of ducks below, she noticed an awful stink. Then she sensed, rather than heard, something behind her. She began to turn, her heart leaping in fright for the second time in less than a minute.

But she never got her head all the way around. A large, filthy hand closed over her mouth and nose, cutting off the scream that had just begun. She was yanked from her feet and pulled against a cold, cold, body. Freezing hands and arms squeezed her close. She could barely breathe, much less scream for help. The smell was terrible. Then she was being carried swiftly along the trail, away from her parents.

CHAPTER ONE

"WHAT'S THIS ABOUT BEING A TRACKER?"

Ranger Shadow Fletcher normally enjoyed watching well-built women as they jogged or ran, even when they were sweaty and their hair in disarray. But as he watched this woman through the glass doors of the Breaks Interstate Park Visitor Center, he quickly decided something must be wrong. She staggered, apparently near exhaustion, as she ran across the parking lot, and her face wore a worried expression. He rose from his chair and went around the counter, intending to open the door.

The woman reached the entrance before him, however, and shoved the door open, bringing in a gust of spring mountain air, crisp with just a hint of pine. Momentarily blinded by the transition from bright sun to indoor lighting, she looked around frantically until her eyes settled on Shadow's dark green ranger's uniform, then rose to his face. She was too upset to give him the curious stare he often received on first meetings. Many people took H. A. Shadow Fletcher, six feet tall and stocky, for an eastern European—some sort of Slav, maybe. He had high cheekbones and his short hair had the black sheen of a Native American, but his dark skin was set off by startling, aquamarine blue eyes, passed down by a Scottish ancestor. One of his old marine buddies had said he looked like the once-popular film star, Charles Bronson, but not as good looking—more like an Ayrab who was a quart low.

"Lost child," she gasped. "Need help."

"Who and where?" Shadow took the woman's arm to steady her. Blue-eyed, long blonde hair pulled back in a ponytail that was now breaking free, she had a lean, taut physique and appeared to be in her mid-thirties. Her tee shirt, with a picture of Mount Rushmore on the front, was soaked with sweat even though the day was cool. Her feet were clad in lightweight hiking shoes and he noted that her

1

legs and arms were cut and scraped.

"My daughter. . ." She wheezed, "down by Grassy Creek – on the trail there. She was ahead of us on the trail, but then she. . ., she. . ."

He pulled a chair from the wall. "Here, sit down and catch your breath"

The woman glanced and the chair and shook her head, taking a deep breath. "Please. We need to go find her. Now."

"How long ago since you last saw her?"

"A couple of hours ago, I guess."

He became aware of Karen McCoy, the other ranger manning the visitor center, standing beside him as her hand thrust out a paper cup of water toward the woman. "Here, drink this, Mrs. . .?"

"Bledsoe," the woman said, taking the water and gulping it.

"Fletcher," McCoy said, "you call the chief at his residence. I'll fill out a missing persons report."

Shadow felt a momentary annoyance at her brusque manner, even though she was senior to him, but quickly realized that the important thing was to find the missing girl. He went back behind the counter, adjusted his thumb, and lifted the receiver with his prosthetic left hand. Consulting a list of telephone numbers thumb-tacked to the wall, he dialed up the cell number for Stanley Martin, the head ranger at The Breaks.

A woman answered the phone. "Yes?"

"This is Ranger Fletcher, at the visitor center. I need to talk to Mr. Martin right away."

"He's in the back yard," came the reply. "I'll get him."

As Shadow waited, he watched McCoy ease Mrs. Bledsoe into a chair. Karen McCoy was a hazel-eyed, slender brunette, maybe thirty, thirty-five, he figured. Her voice had a southern twang that he found charming, even though she'd maintained a distant manner the few times they'd worked together. He knew she was single, had a pre-teen daughter and lived only a couple of doors from him in the tiny community of rangers' residences.

"Try to calm down a bit," she told Mrs. Bledsoe. "I know how upset you are, but it'll take a few minutes to get a search organized."

McCoy went to a table in the small office, came back with a sheet of paper and pulled another chair over to sit beside the other woman. "I need to ask you a few questions while we wait." She grabbed a thick tourist brochure from a nearby rack and set it on her knee to use as a writing support. Taking a pen from her shirt pocket, she laid the sheet of paper, a missing persons report, on it. "Your full name."

"Cleo Bledsoe."

"Spelling?"

"B-L-E-D-S-O-E."

"Address?"

As Mrs. Bledsoe answered McCoy's questions, Shadow chafed at the bit. If he'd been in charge, the report would have waited for later. He would have headed out the door to wherever the little girl had last been seen, leaving the other ranger to deal with the distraught mother.

"Your daughter's name?" asked McCoy.

"Caitlin."

"Age?"

"Ten. She's blonde, same shade as me, but her hair is short. She was wearing red shorts, a Sponge Bob tee shirt and sneakers. She's about four-foot-five and seventy pounds."

As McCoy filled those details onto the form in front of her, Shadow leaned over the counter with a small map of the park and handed it to the woman. "Where did you see her last?" he asked. He needed to know because, as soon as he was off the phone, he was going to be high-tailing it out on the trail in search of that girl.

Mrs. Bledsoe looked up with a start, as if she had forgotten he was there. Then she turned her tear-filled eyes down to the map. "Right about here," she said. "We'd just come out above the creek and begun to follow it."

Shadow was a bit vague about that area of the park; he'd been assigned here only a few weeks ago. It was craggy, rugged country, where you often traveled farther in elevation than distance.

"Isn't that a pretty rough trail for a ten-year-old?" he asked.

The woman shook her head. "Not Caitlin. We've hiked all over the country and she's kept up since she was seven, more or less. Her sister, Emily, is a year younger and she's still out there with my husband, looking."

Shadow asked, "What exactly happened? How did you lose touch with her?"

Mrs. Bledsoe sniffed and wiped tears from her cheeks. "She'd gone ahead, probably because she'd been complaining that Emily was making so much noise that she'd never get to see any animals. She went around a bend in the trail and, when we got there, there was no sign of her. Oh, if only I hadn't left my phone in the RV." She buried her face in her hands.

"Don't worry," McCoy said, putting her hand on the other woman's knee. "We'll find her. She couldn't have gone far, not in these mountains."

Mrs. Bledsoe raised her head and attempted a smile. "I know you'll find her. Thank you."

"Is there anything else that might help us to ident. . . to find her?"

"No. Oh, wait. She always wears a bracelet made out of macaroni bits that her best friend made for her in church camp last year. It's blue and red."

A voice came to Shadow's ear. "Martin, here. Is there a problem?"

"We've got a lost child," said Shadow. "Out on the River Trail, near Grassy Creek. Last seen two maybe hours ago."

"Wait, let me grab a pen," Martin replied.

"Are you camping in the park or staying at the lodge?" Shadow heard McCoy ask.

"Camping," answered Mrs. Bledsoe. "We've got our RV in Campground C."

"Okay, shoot," Martin said over the phone.

"Ten years old, name is Caitlin Bledsoe. Blonde, blue eyes, wearing shorts, a Sponge Bob tee shirt and sneakers."

"Okay," the chief ranger said. "Hmmm, red shorts, huh? That ought to make her easier to spot in the woods. I'll be there in a few minutes and start setting up a search."

Shadow was too impatient to wait. "Let me go on ahead. If I can get out there right away, maybe I can pick up some sign and track her down." He'd had a vague sense of unease ever since arriving at the park and he had a hunch this disappearance might have something to do with it. He'd sensed supernatural presences before, but only in close proximity. This aura seemed to hang in the mountain air.

There was a slight hesitation from Martin. "That's right. You're supposed to be some kind of a professional tracker or something, aren't you?"

Shadow, grinning wryly, could imagine what the chief ranger was thinking: *First they send me some weird-looking Scottish-Indian who's almost brand-new as a ranger, got in some kind of ruckus with the folks at state HQ and now he's pretending he's the last of the Mohicans or something.*

"Well, I don't have an official 'tracker's license,'" he said. "I'm not even sure there is such a thing as a professional tracker. But I grew up hunting and I had a good teacher."

Shadow had been raised in the woods around the Chesapeake Bay in eastern Virginia. His grandfather, Frank Hovering Eagle Fletcher, of Scottish and Virginia Indian ancestry, had been an avid hunter who had passed along his foraging skills and knowledge of wildlife lore to Shadow. Grandfather had been thoroughly based in reality and the Baptist Church.

It was Grandmother Min, however, who had named him and raised him with her usual eccentric flair. She swore to be a full-blooded Accomattoc Indian even though the tribe was officially extinct, for she saw things with a different eye, perhaps an inner one. Although she attended church with her husband, she'd taught young Shadow to be free in his beliefs of spiritual things.

In other words, Grandfather had indoctrinated him in the Baptist ways while Grandmother taught him how not to be Baptist.

"I don't know why we need a tracker," Martin said. "We'll have a search party in there pretty quick."

"That's the problem, Chief. If there *are* any tracks to be found, they'll be wiped out once a gang of men has traipsed through there."

"That's right," Martin said tentatively. "They did say something about you finding a missing woman at your last park." He hesitated. "Who's on duty with you?"

"McCoy."

"She knows the park as good as anyone. Have her head out there and you stay at the center with the mother."

"But Mr. Martin, I'm the man to send out there. I. . ."

"No buts. You're new here, Fletcher. You remain there—no wait. Is the

4

child's family staying here in the park?"

"Yes, Campground C, but. . ."

"Do this," the chief ranger said, "Lock the visitor center up for a few minutes. Take the woman back to her campsite and get a recent picture of the child if she has one, then take her to the office. I'll meet you there in a few minutes."

Martin hung up and Shadow saw that McCoy was staring at him. "What's this about being a tracker?"

"Well, yeah. My grandfather taught me and I hunt a lot."

"You ever hunt in the mountains?"

"Well, no. Not these mountains. But I've. . ."

"You're a flatlander. All we got up here is coal and rocks. Little rocks piled on big rocks, big rocks piled on bigger rocks, the whole mess on a huge field of coal with mines running deep into it. You can't track across rock."

"Of course you can," he insisted. How the hell did this hillbilly know what he could or couldn't do?

McCoy snorted. "Well, I don't have time to argue. What did Martin say to do?"

"He said," Shadow kept his voice level, "for me to take Mrs. Bledsoe to get a picture of her daughter and take her to the office. You're to lock up and go start the search." He took Mrs. Bledsoe's elbow, and ushered her toward the door. "So I'd better be going, hadn't I?"

Once outside, he opened the passenger door of his small, green Ford pickup for Mrs. Bledsoe, then went around and slid behind the wheel. "What campsite are you in, Ma'am?" he asked.

"C-11," she said. "But why can't I go with the other ranger? I have to help her look—to show her where we last saw Caitlin."

He started the engine and pulled away from the office, then looked over and gave her his best reassuring smile. "Ma'am, I doubt your daughter could get far off the trail, that's rugged country. What if she finds her way onto the trail again and comes back to your RV? Actually, she might be there now, since you've been searching for quite a while. Let's go check."

"Oh. I never thought of that. It would be a long way for her to walk alone, but. . ."

Despite the urgency he felt, Shadow forced himself to drive slowly because, as in any park, there were a few kids running around, mostly chasing each other and screaming, and they tended to run out in the road from the underbrush or from behind travel trailers and campers.

It was a sunny Saturday in early April, the first full weekend that the park's campgrounds were open. Most of the sites in the park's three campgrounds were occupied; every nice-weather weekend brought throngs of campers to The Breaks, where Americans could commune with nature.

Yet, instead of the chirping melodies of birds calling from branches on high, Shadow heard snatches of music and television shows coming from the open windows of trailers and motor homes. He couldn't smell the fresh air that everyone came to the mountains for. Woodsmoke and exhaust fumes filled the air, and every once in a while he got a whiff of the campgrounds' sewage systems, where campers could empty their vehicles' holding tanks.

Not for the first time, he wondered why anyone would want to spend a weekend or more in a crowded, smelly, noisy RV park. They'd put out big money to spend weekends camping in these rigs, yet he'd bet these very same people would look down on folks who lived in trailer parks in the small Kentucky town at the base of the mountain.

"That's our RV there." Mrs. Bledsoe pointed out a blue and white medium-sized vehicle with an awning that extended over a portable table and chairs.

Shadow pulled over. "Go make sure she's not there. And see if you have a recent photo of her."

When she had disappeared into the RV, he ran his hand through his short hair and reached into a small bag of jellybeans he always kept in a shirt pocket. He tended to snack on sweets, in lieu of the cigarettes he'd smoked for so many years. He'd been overweight and a bit flabby from his hospital stay until he'd begun the demanding, physical work of a park ranger. But now, in this park, he was more of a "let-me-tell-you-about-the-park's-history" desk jockey, and was beginning to put on a few pounds again.

He was getting the hang of "The Claw," though. When he'd first been fitted with the prosthetic device, he'd had a hard time holding a beer can without dropping it. Now he had no problem with beer at all. He could even use a key to unlock a door. And he was getting to be more coordinated with his right hand, too. He'd been a "lefty" before he'd had a brief encounter with a suicide bomber.

The Claw consisted of four plastic bendable fingers across from a passive thumb. Even though he had no direct control over the thumb, he could reach over with his right hand and position it for a wider or narrower grip – the difference between holding a key or a beer can. The fingers, with polyethylene fiber strings running inside jointed digits, would close and bend with a flex of his wrist muscles, which had been surgically altered to allow him to pull. The whole affair was covered with realistic, latex "skin" over soft foam that gave the contraption the right shape, a mirror image of his right, real, hand.

The door of the RV opened again almost immediately and Mrs. Bledsoe jumped down, not bothering with the steps. Her face, Shadow noticed, was still red—not from exertion, but sunburn.

"She's not here," she said, eyes moist. "But here's the picture, she's the one with a hat on."

"Don't worry, we'll find her," Shadow said. "Let's get you to the office so we can get the ball rolling."

Looking at the photo, he saw Mrs. Bledsoe and her two daughters posing with a dog, probably taken by the husband. He put it in his shirt pocket and drove to the park office, just across the road from the visitor center where he'd started. It was behind the Laurel Lodge's restaurant, where the smell of garbage seeped from the dumpsters. At least that was better than the outhouses at the last park where he'd worked. Nowhere near as primitive as his last assignment, this park boasted many modern amenities besides modern toiletry, not the least of these being the many buildings and cottages making up the lodge, which was on the lip of The Breaks, a huge rift in the mountains billed as, "The Grand Canyon of the South."

He took Mrs. Bledsoe up the stairs and showed her into the office. Chief Ranger Martin was there, talking to three other rangers. In his forties, probably not much older than Shadow, his face was wrinkled and leathery, framed by hair so gray that it appeared white. Although thin, with an ass flat as a washboard, he had shoulders that seemed to go backward and a belly sticking out like he was carrying a volleyball beneath his shirt. A long neck, receding chin, beak nose and protruding eyes made him appear rooster-like.

He glanced over, but finished giving instructions for areas to be searched before turning to the newcomers as the rangers left for their assignments. "Mrs. Bledsoe?"

She nodded.

"Try not to worry. Your daughter is probably on or near one of the trails. It's very difficult to get around off-trail." Martin said, and then turned to Shadow. "You have a photo?"

Shadow handed it over.

"Where's the missing persons report?" Martin took out reading glasses and peered at the picture.

"Uh… Ranger McCoy filled it out. I guess it's still over at the visitor center."

"Well, when you get back there, fax it over to me."

"Back there? Aren't we going to close the center so I can help in the search?"

"You're new here, Fletcher. I run a tight operation. By the book. The visitor center is supposed to be open every day from nine to five. I've already made two exceptions by closing it long enough for you to get a picture of the child and letting McCoy leave her normal duties."

"But the little girl. . ."

Martin's answer was crisp. "I've sent several rangers out there already and I'm calling in those who were off duty. I expect we'll have found her by five. If not, you'll be expected to join in the search then."

"Yes, sir." Shadow turned and left.

When he returned to the visitor center, he faxed the report, then turned up the volume on the park radio and listened to calls between rangers as the search went on. The father and sister were quickly located, but they found no sign of the missing girl. The rest of the afternoon dragged by. Only a few people came to the center, wandered through the small museum on the other side of the lobby from the counter and asked a few questions. Mostly he sat behind the counter, studying a detailed map of the park while popping jellybeans into his mouth and sucking them slowly.

At five, he quickly closed up and got in his truck. A half-mile later, he pulled into the parking lot for the State Line Overlook. He got out, folded the rear of the truck's seat forward, and grabbed his emergency backpack, which contained things such as a first-aid kit, a couple of bottles of store-bought water, a waterproof windbreaker, a lightweight emergency blanket' a waterproof pack of matches, extra flashlight batteries and other sundry items. On impulse, since he hadn't eaten lunch, he stuffed some candy bars from the glove compartment into the pack.

He straightened, put on the pack, and slung a small pair binoculars around his neck—his eyesight was extraordinary, but vast distances were common here. Clipping a portable radio onto his gunbelt, he started down the trail. And "down" the trail, in this park, really meant steep. The park's buildings, campgrounds and facilities were on the mostly flat top of a peak. Cliffs dropped off the edges of this area of the park, giving scenic views of the surrounding countryside, including the neighboring state of Kentucky.

Taking a small detour down a set of man-made steps, he came out atop the State Line Overlook. This was an outcropping where a stone wall had been built overlooking the Russell Fork River, which had carved out The Breaks. From here, atop one of the many huge rock crags jutting out of the mountainside, he had an aerial view and could study the area to be searched. The Breaks was billed as an "interstate" park because it straddled the state line between Kentucky and Virginia.

A thousand feet below him, at the bottom of the canyon, the river rippled swiftly over rocks, although he could only see a portion of it. On the other side of the chasm, on a natural rock shelf a couple of hundred feet above the river, the Old Clinchfield Railroad snaked along and then plunged into the clearly visible maw of the State Line Tunnel, the square-cut rocks that formed the entry arch giving it the appearance of a medieval battlement. The railway had been built at the beginning of the twentieth century to carry coal out of the mountains and was still in use. But that was on the other side of the river, far from where Caitlin Bledsoe had disappeared, so he concentrated on the nearer portion of the canyon floor.

The seasonal trees had barely begun to leaf out, so most of the canyon showed bare to his inspection. Massive, weathered gray towers of rock rose from the floor of the gorge and even the sides of some cliffs. At this distance, he didn't bother with the binoculars. If there were anyone out in the open, he'd see them.

He wasn't completely familiar with the lay of the land, and couldn't see the waters of Grassy Creek from here, but he knew about where to look. He saw no one, not the girl nor any of the searchers.

From here Shadow had a choice. He could either turn left and follow the steeply descending River Trail and follow it downstream to the mouth of Grassy Creek or opt for taking the Ridge Trail to the more gradual Laurel Branch Trail, the path taken earlier by the Bledsoes. He supposed the latter might provide a chance to memorize the track of Caitlin's shoes. It would also be quicker, and that ever-present sense of foreboding urged him on. He turned his radio off, so he wouldn't be distracted by the chatter of other searchers, and set off.

Soon he was panting. He'd begun to sweat, too. It seemed almost warm out here on the mountainside, despite having the snow flurries last night. The Bledsoe family must be used to hiking, he decided, to have decided to take this trail. Or, on second thought, they might be like a lot of folks unaccustomed to the mountains, overconfident. Then again, Shadow wasn't used to this up-and-down travel, either. When he reached the Laurel Branch trail, he went left.

He hiked through a mixed forest of hemlocks and hardwoods. There were thickets of evergreen rhododendron and laurel choking the spaces between the trunks. Every once in a while, he'd see a splash of blue paint on a tree trunk near the trail—markers to keep inexperienced hikers on track.

He soon came to the sign where the Laurel Branch Trail turned into the Grassy Creek Trail. It was a steep downhill slope now, only navigable by staying on the switchbacks of the trail.

Watching the ground for sign, he gradually became aware that someone followed him. Maybe he was catching sight of movement above and behind him from the corners of his eyes or hearing slight sounds out of the ordinary, or perhaps merely the feeling of being watched tipped him off, but somebody was back there. He turned and scanned the slopes above him, catching a glimpse of something disappearing behind a boulder, as if someone had ducked out of sight.

Stopping, he stood and waited for a couple of minutes, expecting someone to appear again farther along the trail, but it didn't happen. The follower hung back, not trying to catch up, but shadowing him. Turning, he went on. Slipping and sliding, he descended the mountainside a quickly as he could, hoping to gain distance on his pursuer, for no other reason than being nervous about having someone on his back trail.

But then he realized he had been distracted into paying more attention to the person behind him than looking for Caitlin Bledsoe and that made him angry. Evening was drawing on and sunset would come early as the sun dropped below the western peaks. It would be rough on a child to spend a night on the slopes in near-freezing temperatures.

He thought about his own daughter, Ashley. He hadn't seen her in weeks, and that had been just a short afternoon visit. Well, there was a custody hearing coming up in a couple of weeks and then maybe he'd be able to spend more time with her. After all that mess at False Cape Park—and he'd nearly gotten himself killed there, a couple of times—Shadow had decided to straighten matters out and clear up his good name, once and for all. He'd gotten a lawyer, who had arranged for a review of the custody decree.

Shadow picked up the pace again, sweating heavily now. He wasn't used to such strenuous hiking, being accustomed to the flat lands in the eastern part of the state. He thought about taking a breather, but he was uneasy about doing that if someone was spying on him. Then again, why not? Arriving at a place where he could watch the trail above him, he removed his backpack, took a drink from a water bottle, and then selected a candy bar. It wasn't a chocolate bar, but one of the sweet, nutty bars touted for energy.

He waited. If it were just a harmless hiker or another searcher behind him, he'd catch up to Shadow after a few minutes.

His shadow didn't show himself, so he went on, again moving quickly. He didn't pause when he came to Grassy Creek, still quite a ways below him. The trail turned left to follow the water, descending gently now. Shadow's pursuer would lose the advantage of being on higher ground.

After a bit, the trail leveled out and he was on a ledge that would take him around one of the large, jutting rock formations. Instead, he stepped behind a smaller crag and waited. Anyone after him would assume he had turned the corner and gone out of sight.

It wasn't long until he heard someone coming slowly along. Probably easing up on the bend to be sure Shadow had gone far enough ahead to be safe. When the footsteps came almost abreast of his hiding place, he stepped out, his hand on the butt of his pistol.

CHAPTER TWO

"WHAT TOOK YOU SO LONG?"

Karen McCoy gasped in surprise and stepped back.

Shadow felt a surge of anger. "McCoy? Why the hell are you sneaking up on me?"

"Whew, you gave me a fright. I was about to start another sweep of the area, when I saw you coming down the trail." She grinned, somewhat maliciously. "I wanted to see a real tracker in action, so I followed."

"What the hell for? You got nothing better to do than play games when a little girl is missing?"

"Do you?" Her grin quickly turned into an obvious sneer. "Look, Fletcher. I didn't appreciate what you pulled back there. I heard that bull you told Martin about tracking and it's a load of hogwash. You were just trying to get a chance to come out here ahead of me."

"No, really," he said. "I knew that if a search party got here before me, I'd have a harder time picking up that little girl's trail."

"I doubt you'll be able to track her anyway. This is goldang rocky, hard-to-get-around-in country; even Daniel Boone gave up on traveling through here. They didn't have any roads in here until the 'fifties.'"

"You might be surprised what I can track," Shadow said. "But we're wasting time."

"So where do we start, Dan'l?"

"We?" He raised an eyebrow. "I didn't know we were partners." Then he grinned wryly. "Who knows, maybe we will make a team. You know the park better, where do you think we should start?"

She smiled in turn. "Dang right I know the park better. You wouldn't know a lick from a holler. I talked to the father earlier; the girl was last seen just a couple of hundred yards down the trail from where we are now. But I've already circled up and down this trail twice, along with a passel of other folks. Might just as well start right here."

"Suits me," Shadow said. But let me go ahead of you if you don't mind."

"Make sense. You're supposed to be the tracker."

"That's what we're about to establish," he said.

They hiked on a nearly gentle slope now that they traveled beside the river. He watched the ground to his left, paying attention to the lay of the land.

Most of the ground beneath his feet, as McCoy had warned, was rock. The only place he saw much trace of recent passage was in some of the moss growing in the shade of overhanging rocks. Short-lived indistinct scuffles showing partial footprints. Nevertheless, he watched such areas carefully; they were the best chance he had.

Suddenly, just before the trail turned to the left around a large overhanging rock that nearly formed a tunnel, he stopped. Something was very wrong.

"What do you see?"

McCoy's voice from behind seemed to come from a great distance. Evil washed over Shadow and he knew, with no evidence from his physical senses, that something evil had been here, the force he'd been feeling for a few days now.

He'd felt such a malevolent presence before. It had long ago appeared—if appeared was the right word for something you couldn't see—whenever Grandmother Min, for whatever reason of her own, would call on the darker side of Indian mysticism. And he'd sensed it again recently, when a psychotic killer had teamed up with a Native American spirit to murder several people, including one of Shadow's friends.

Shadow had never been able to name the emotion he felt in the face of supernatural wickedness, but he compared it to coming on a rattlesnake without warning. Even though he had no phobia about snakes, and no matter that the reptile was not in striking range, some primeval network of nerves filled him with an urge to be in some other part of the landscape as soon as possible.

But there was something different about this particular aura. A new sensation. An icy tingling of the nerves and skin that said he could never run far enough away to be safe from this eerie presence.

"Wait here," he said softly, drawing his pistol. Evil itself could not harm him. But he'd learned that wickedness was usually connected with a human. A wolf or cougar waiting around that bend wouldn't emanate evil; it would only be acting according to its nature. And if that malevolent force came from a man, a bullet would be Shadow's best protection. He crept forward and went around the corner, staying as far away from the rock as he could.

His gun pointed at a fissure in the rock, almost a cave. The grotto, large enough to easily conceal two men, wasn't dark, though, since it faced directly into the descending sun. It was empty.

Forcing himself to ignore the fear evoked by the supernatural aura coming from the cleft, he holstered his gun. He jumped as a voice sounded from close behind. "What did you see?" In his concentration he'd nearly forgotten McCoy.

"Nothing," he said. "Just spooked I guess. But there's something about that gap in the rock."

He stepped closer. The bottom of the opening was nearly flat and a deposit of wind-blown leaves had composted down into a soft soil, sprinkled with white flecks of snow that had not melted in the shadows. And that loam had recently been disturbed. Someone had stood in that hole-in-the-wall. He bent over and peered in. There was a hint of foul odor.

It wasn't much as far as tracks go, just a shallow heel imprint. An amateur might have taken it for a partial bear track, but Shadow knew bear walked flat-footed, never leaving a heel print. And there wasn't room for a bear inside that depression unless it was standing on its hind legs, which was highly improbable. So something with very large feet had stood in that hollow recently—a man no doubt.

But that brought up another puzzle. Nowhere could he see a curve regular enough to make him think shoes or boots were involved. No, this large-footed man had been barefoot, or maybe wearing moccasins. And barefoot was out of the question in this rock-strewn area. Moccasins, then.

He'd learned all he could from the physical evidence, but a good tracker didn't stop there. The habits of the animal being tracked might be of invaluable use on a faint trail. Would a bear go for the grove or the clearing? Would the doe and fawn cross a river or walk along the bank? So, in this case, what would a man standing in that fissure be up to?

Ambush. But, although it was a hiding place, it wasn't a very good one; anyone coming down the trail would have seen a person in that little niche. Unless. . . Shadow looked to the west, where the sun was halfway down the sky. Right now, the hole-in-the-wall was obvious, but in late morning? It would have been in shadows, and the sun would have been in the eyes of someone coming down the trail. Which made the tiny cavern a good place for an ambush. And ambush meant predator.

"Look, there at the back," he said. "What do you see?"

She came up and leaned down next to him, their shoulders touching. "Nothing," she said after a moment. "What am I looking for?"

He pointed the print out to her. "That's a heel print. Somebody stood in this opening. Somebody very large, from the size of it."

"So? Maybe the girl, Caitlin, was spying on her family, playing a game."

"No, this was an adult, not a kid. And I see no reason for someone to hide in there that doesn't seem a bit sinister to me."

"You're not kidding are you? You really see a track there?"

She couldn't see the imprint, Shadow realized, because she wasn't accustomed to looking closely. Same reason that she couldn't feel the menacing aura that enveloped them, her senses weren't attuned to it. Maybe she'd have been able to discern the print earlier, but it had been hours and the spongy leaf debris had sprung back up, somewhat. Time wasted before tracking began was game lost, thought Shadow, mentally cursing the chief ranger for his earlier decision. Would there be enough trail-sign left?

"We'd better move along," Shadow said. "Maybe there's more sign farther on."

The next break came a few hundred feet farther on. A small tree angled out over the slope leading down to the creek. He pointed it out to McCoy.

"So how do you know the tree didn't just grow crooked?" she asked when he told her someone had bent the sapling.

"No, it's straight at the bottom and there's a couple of cracks where the bark split with the strain. And the leaves and branches would have grown to compensate if it had grown crooked, straining for direct sunlight." He gestured at the rugged country around them. "Especially here where the sun comes up late and goes down early because it's in a canyon."

"Maybe the girl fell and grabbed onto it."

"No, someone heavy used it for balance going off the edge. Maybe carrying something, grabbed it with one hand for balance." He leaned his head out over the ledge. "Then he climbed down this slope, there's scuffing and a few pebbles have been dislodged. A few hours ago, maybe. But why leave an easy trail that leads down to the creek to climb down a slope to reach the same creek?"

"To avoid being seen?"

"Good guess." He looked back up the trail. "If whoever-it-was heard people coming around that bend, he could duck out of sight. And remember what the mother said about the younger daughter making a lot of noise."

"So you think that. . ."

But Shadow ignored her. Turning about, he began descending the steep slope, parallel to the marks he was following, so as not to disturb them. He was on the hunt now.

As he went down, he was dimly aware that McCoy followed. He watched for any footprint or even a partial print, but didn't hope for any. The ground was too hard. The trail wasn't too difficult to follow, though, he noticed several dislodged pebbles. Then he came to the creek.

There was a bit of a beach, just a narrow strip of pebbles to walk upon. Two weeks earlier, Shadow guessed, the stream would have been swollen and running swiftly though the gorge. There'd have been no beach at all then.

"Stay here," he told McCoy when she arrived at his side. To his surprise, she didn't argue.

He went upstream first, since that was the direction his quarry had been traveling when still up on the trail. Dropping to his knees, he watched for overturned pebbles, both on the bank and on the streambed. Nothing. He went back to where McCoy waited, then repeated the process downstream. Again he found no sign.

"He didn't go upstream or down that I can tell," he told her when he returned the second time. "So he probably went across."

He sat down and began removing his shoes and socks. Not that he was squeamish about getting his shoes wet; wet footwear might cause blisters if he had to walk any distance afterward.

"So you'll pick up his trail on the other side?" She also sat down and removed her footwear.

"No need for you to come along," he said. "It'll be rugged going."

"I'm going with you."

"Suit yourself."

They waded into the crystal-clear waters, walking gingerly on the rocky bottom. Ice-cold water swirled about their lower legs, soaking their uniform trousers. Many of the rocks were smooth and slippery. He checked the beach again, directly opposite. There was nothing to show their quarry might have left the water here. He walked upstream, followed by McCoy, then stopped thirty yards farther on. An unnatural shape, floating in an eddy on the edge of the creek, had caught his eye. Bending, he saw a soggy piece of pasta, formed like a slightly curved tube. It was blue, as though colored by food dye. He picked it up with his hand and laid it out on the palm of the The Claw. McCoy gasped and put one hand over her mouth when she saw it.

"He went upriver," Shadow said.

"How can you tell?"

"If we'd found it downstream, it wouldn't tell much. But nothing floats upstream against this much current."

"Oh."

"Hold this," Shadow said. "It's evidence, I guess. If you have a tissue or something, wrap it up."

He took the radio from his belt, turned it on, and thumbed the switch.

"Fletcher to Martin."

The reply came immediately. "Go ahead, this is Martin,"

"I'd advise you to put out an Amber Alert, Chief."

"Based on what?"

"I've found evidence that makes me sure she's been abducted." Shadow replied.

"Where are you?"

"Ranger McCoy and I are below the River Trail, where Grassy Creek meets the river."

"Wait there," the Chief Ranger ordered.

Damn it! He hit the transmit switch. "Chief Martin, I need to keep on the trail. It'll be dark soon.

"You heard me, Fletcher. You wait right there.

John Bushore

CHAPTER THREE

"WAS YOU EVER MARRIED, SHADDER?"

"You've got to be kidding." The chief ranger looked down at the piece of pasta in his hand. He was standing at the edge of the creek with Shadow and McCoy. "You want me to put out an Amber Alert based on a noodle and a few scuff marks?"

"I know it's not much to go on," said Shadow. "But the girl didn't just wander off. Someone grabbed her, and brought her down here to the creek."

"You don't know that for a fact. She could have been walking along the river, slipped and broken her bracelet. Hell, it could have washed downstream from God knows where."

McCoy spoke up. "Stanley, I believe him. He seemed to know what he's doing. He brought us straight here."

Martin shook his head. "It doesn't wash, Karen. Why would someone abduct a child from here? This isn't a playground or something; there aren't that many kids out on these trails. Then he'd have to carry her if he took her back up the trail to his car. It's quite a hike and someone would have seen them."

"What's out there?" Shadow waved northwest.

"Nothing until you get to Highway 80," McCoy answered.

"It's damn near straight up," Martin said. "And there's no trail."

"I know it doesn't make sense," Shadow admitted. "But someone came down that slope from the trail in a hurry, heading that way. I'd put money on it."

"Or maybe the girl fell down that slope." Martin wrapped the macaroni noodle back up and put it in his pocket. "And it's my butt that'll be at stake if I cry wolf. An Amber Alert covers several states, for God's sake."

Shadow saw a flashlight beam move off in the distance, back up near the River Trail. The rangers hadn't stopped searching at sunset, and now more and more volunteers were showing up to help. It was turning cold, near freezing. "And if she *was* abducted?" he asked.

"You haven't convinced me of that—not by a long shot."

"But she might have left. . ."

"No buts. If you don't like my decision, get out there and find something to change my mind." Martin turned and made his way upstream, to where the search was being conducted.

"Damn it," muttered Shadow. There was no chance of showing the chief ranger the signs he'd found, not in the dark. And, since McCoy couldn't see the signs, neither would Martin.

"He's a good man," McCoy said. "And you shouldn't curse. He just can't believe anything so horrible as a kidnapping could happen here. There's never been much crime around here, unless you count moonshinin'."

"Moonshining? They still do that?"

"Sure, it's good money and it sort of gets passed down from pappy to son. Beats the heck out of workin' for a living."

"Well, I think we're talking about something much more serious than making a little hootch." He turned and started downstream.

"Where you goin'?" she asked.

"Gonna try to pick up the trail."

"In the dark?"

"I've got a flashlight," he said. "You got any better suggestions?"

"Yeah, I'll go with you."

"No need."

"Like crap." McCoy turned on her flash. "You don't know these hills. You'll get lost."

"Not likely. But I'll take you up on the offer. Thanks, McCoy."

"Call me Karen, would you? If you don't mind me callin' you Shadder."

He grinned in the dark. No one had ever pronounced his name that way before but, then again, he'd never been addressed by a true "hillbilly."

"Karen it is," he said. "Let's go."

*

Shadow trudged into his house late Sunday morning. The searchers hadn't seen hide or hair of the Bledsoe girl, and he'd failed to find where the abductor's trail left the creek. Tracking in these rocky chasms was difficult, despite his bravado when talking to Karen. He'd probably never have seen the first sign, in the rock fissure, if it hadn't been for that eerie sensation.

And what about that? Every other time he'd experienced such a thing, it had its roots in Native American mysticism. This disappearance certainly didn't have anything to do with Indian religion. But, maybe, just maybe if it had been a pedophile, such a crime might be despicable enough for him to sense the wrongness of it without any ties to aboriginal culture. Anyway, he was too tired to worry about it now.

He threw his windbreaker over a chair, slipped out of his gun belt and boots, then went into the bathroom to brush his teeth. The inside of his mouth felt scummy from the candy he'd shared with Karen during the night's search, unwilling to break off the quest to go back for food. Returning to the bedroom, he set the alarm to go off in five hours, then lay back and slept.

*

Shadow had just finished a can of pork and beans and was making a couple of sandwiches when someone knocked on his kitchen door. Only one person used the back door—the only person ever to have visited him at all, actually. "Come on in, Jack."

John Goodluck filled the doorframe as he walked in. Known as Shawnee Jack, he stood several inches over six feet and weighed maybe two-fifty. He wore civvies, a checkered shirt over worn jeans and a belt with a silver-dollar buckle. Attached to that belt was a large, bone-handled hunting knife in a leather sheath. Straight, shiny black hair, worn over his shoulders to nearly mid-back, accented scowling Indian features, which rarely showed a smile.

He and Shadow had begun playing cribbage in the evening once in a while, lately, with Shadow drinking beer and Jack tossing back glasses of Jack Daniels and coke. Card playing was the only interest they shared, Jack's other two passions being Shawnee history and woman chasing.

"I was out looking for ceremonial sites," Jack said without greeting, stopping just inside the door. "I heard there's a kid missing, on my truck radio."

"Yeah, ten-year-old named Caitlin Bledsoe. No sign of her so far."

"Where was she last seen?"

"Grassy Creek trail." Shadow held out the loaf of bread. "I'm on my way back out there. Just packing some chow to take along. We're going to search by the highway. You want to come along?"

"Sure, toss a sandwich or two in for me. No mustard, though. Be right back." Jack slipped out.

A few minutes later, he reappeared in his battered, yellow Jeep Wrangler as Shadow tossed his backpack in the back of the Ranger. Now wearing his uniform, Jack jumped out, scooped up Shadow's pack and threw it in his own vehicle. "No way." He pointed at the Jeep's passenger seat. "I'm not playing sardine in that little truck of yours."

Shadow shrugged and stepped up into the 4 by 4. He didn't have to open a door; there weren't any. It was a convertible but the top was folded back. It always sounded like it had a hole in the muffler and the brakes screeched whenever they were applied. With a roar and a spurt of tires on gravel, they were off.

"I take it this was your weekend off?" Shadow asked.

"Told you that last week. Another senior moment?"

"Screw you." Shadow was more than a decade older. "So you lookin' for caves again?"

"Yeah." Jack was passionate about finding caves, used by the Shawnee for hundreds of years. Besides being treasure troves of artifacts, they had a deep, spiritual meaning to him.

"You're not fooling me," Shadow said. "You're really looking for a gold mine so you can retire to a life of wine, women and song."

19

Jack grunted. "Where do we start?"

"Martin's agreed to let me check out the area along Highway 80 in Kentucky. I'm supposed to meet Karen McCoy at someplace called the Confederate Soldier's Grave. We're going to walk back along the road, then search in the Center Creek area."

"Center Creek?" Jack glanced over. "I was out that way yesterday. Nobody's searched there?"

"Of course," Shadow said. "But they're searching for a lost girl. I'm looking for sign."

"What kind of sign?"

"I think the girl was abducted and taken cross-country to the highway."

"What?" The jeep swerved slightly. "Whatever gave you that idea?"

Shadow told him about the tracks and the macaroni noodle that he'd found.

Jack whistled."My friend, you've told me you could track some and I'm sure you can. But moccasins? Hardly anyone wears moccasins in the mountains."

"You do," Shadow said, looking down at Jack's feet on the pedals.

"Yeah, but only up here in the main part of the park. I put on regular hiking boots when I'm in the hills."

"Well, I've got to admit, the track was pretty faint. Karen saw it, too, but she couldn't make anything out of it. But it was either moccasins or barefoot. There was no sign of a hard heel like a shoe."

Jack turned left onto Highway 80. This road would descend into the same valley that held Grassy Creek, the road meandering along beside and below the highway. When they reached Kentucky, the creek merged with the Russell River and the highway then followed the river. For quite a while, they traveled along the edge of The Breaks, where the park's boundary paralleled the highway. Both men remained silent, Jack concentrating on the twisting road, Shadow looking at the few houses along the road, trying to get a sense of the countryside. Sometimes the houses would be high above them, perched on a fairly level shelf of rock on the mountainside. At other times, Shadow could look directly down on roofs and chimneys of shacks and trailers tucked into small hollows along the creek.

Few of these homes looked prosperous. This part of the country had long been impoverished, with little more than coal mines to provide jobs. Nearly every home had a truck garden beside it, where vegetables could be grown for summer consumption and also canned for the long, cold winters. Nothing that he saw—or had seen since his arrival—would account for Shadow's feeling that something was wrong with the place.

They had just gone past some sort of civil war roadside marker and Shadow was studying the few places on the roadside where a car could pull off, when Jack said, "Karen, huh?"

"What?"

"You always called her 'McCoy,' before. And now you're teaming up with her today. Anything going on?"

"Not like you mean. We were on duty in the visitor center when the mother came in to report the missing child."

"Oh, I wouldn't fault you. McCoy's a good-looking woman and it's just not natural for a man to be alone as long as you. Just make sure you don't piss her off. You don't want her taking potshots at you."

"What are you talking about?"

"She's a McCoy, ain't she?"

"And. . .?"

Jack turned and flashed one of his rare grins. "Well, you ain't no Hatfield, but she's still got a temper and she's on the right hand side of God. Don't start any feuds."

"Really? One of those McCoys?"

"Yep, but she doesn't make a big deal about it. Still, this is Pike County, Kaintucky and people still talk about the old feud." Jack hit the brakes. "Here we are."

He turned left into a small parking lot behind a curbed island of landscaped gardens—mostly brown this time of year—surrounding an interstate-green highway marker. Shadow could make out the top line of golden print: KNOWN BUT TO GOD.

Karen stood waiting beside her car, an older model green minivan with peeling paint.

Karen walked over to the jeep and reached the passenger side just as Jack shut off the ignition. "Hey, Shadder," she said without a smile. "I see you brought reinforcements. This the best you could do?"

"I love you, too, McCoy," Jack said. "You were hoping for the cavalry? Like maybe the Seventh?"

Shadow, stuck in the passenger seat between the two, wondered if they were kidding around or if the animosity was for real.

"Cavalry would be better," she said flatly. "You do know your way around these hills, though; I'll give you that. But we're not looking for one of your pretty, park-visitor girlfriends here."

"Give me a break, McCoy." Jack looked off into the distance as though bored. "I never joined your church full of bible-bangers, so I don't have to listen to the sermons."

"You're right," Karen said, her lips tight. "What you do off-duty is none of my business."

"And good day to you, too." Jack swung out of the jeep, reached back in for a pair of hiking boots, and sat down on the running board to change.

Shadow swung a leg out and Karen backed up a step to let him out. He didn't know what to say, so he kept silent. He walked around the jeep and Karen followed.

Jack laced up his boots. "So what's the plan? Or would you rather I just head back and sign on with Martin's group?"

Karen sighed. "No, the more searchers the better, I guess. We're just going to walk back along the shoulder of the road so Shadder can look fer tire tracks on the shoulder or footprints comin' up from the ravine. If somebody took the Bledsoe girl, they musta been headin' for this road."

Jack stood and looked out over the landscape. He rubbed his chin. "If anyone *were* planning to leave the area, they'd have to, wouldn't they?"

"Of course he'd be leaving the area," Shadow said, wishing he could see Jack's face. It had seemed an odd comment to make. "Why would they stay out in the hills?"

"Sorry, just thinking out loud. You folks going to stand around and talk all day, or should we get started?" Jack picked up his moccasins and threw them into the jeep.

"The way I figure it," Shadow said, "there are so few places to pull off the road, we'll have to check both sides." He shouldered his pack. "Jack, you said you were out this way yesterday? You didn't pull off around here, did you?"

"No, why?"

"I'd hate to go off on a wild goose chase after your prints. Anyway, let's get going. Why don't you take the uphill side of the road?"

"You got it."

They started off, Jack walking across the highway and then keeping parallel with them as Shadow and Karen searched for any sign of someone climbing up from the creek bottom to the road. Shadow could see right away that it was a long shot. Most of the drop-offs on their side of the road were so steep that he doubted a mountain goat could climb them. Did they have mountain goats around here, he wondered. Just one more reminder of how little he knew about this part of the world.

Down here, still in the park, there were no campgrounds or lodges on this side. Here, the Russell River itself was the attraction, running just below and paralleling the highway for a couple of miles, an alluring attraction for whitewater rafters. It was quite different from the flat land and lazy waters of his youth.

As though reading his thoughts, Karen asked, "Where you from, Shadder?"

"I was brought up in Virginia, over by Chesapeake Bay." He shrugged. "But I don't call anyplace home. I've always moved around a lot.

"That's right, you're an ex-marine, ain't you?"

"Yeah."

"You retired?"

"Disability." He wondered at the sudden curiosity.

"Oh, that's right—your hand. I forgot."

They walked in silence for a bit, then she asked, "You get to see a lot of the world?"

"Yeah. "

"I always wanted to see the ocean. I never seen it."

He stepped around the end of the guardrail, off the roadway, turning to look at her. "You're kidding."

"Nope. Never been anywheres but here. Sometimes I dreamed of leaving, but I got married just out of high school. Then I never saw any reason to leave after I had my daughter. My husband took off and I got this job as a ranger. The pay ain't great, but I live in a nicer house than I grew up in. And I'm not so far away that I can't go down the mountain on Sundays and go to church with my ma and pa."

"That's nice," Shadow commented while studying a scuffmark.

"Do you ever go to church?"

"Uh, no. Not much."

"The church has meant a lot to me my whole life, 'specially since my man left. It's hard to raise a young 'un up these days by yourself. Was you ever married, Shadder?"

"Um, yeah. Divorced."

"I suppose it would be tough on a woman, her man off to war all the time." She sighed. "If'n I had a husband, I'd want him at home."

Shadow shouted across to Jack. "Finding anything?"

Jack shook his head.

"Nothing here, either." Shadow called, then stepped up onto the roadway and started along the next section of guardrail. "Let's check the next pullover," he said over his shoulder.

They passed a sign saying: <u>Road Surface Crumbling Ahead</u> and soon came upon a place where the roadway had partially washed away beneath, leaving humps and cracks in the asphalt roadway. The guardrail seemed to be on shaky ground, also. Shadow looked both ways, then walked around the rough area.

"Somebody needs to fix this," he said.

"Over in Virginia, they fix them. In Kentucky we put up a sign, figurin' any damn fool can drive around it. When enough of the road goes over the edge, they'll fix it."

"You're from Kentucky, I take it."

"Yep," she answered. "Proud of it."

"I'll bet. Lots of heritage." He was thinking of the feud her family had carried on for years.

"Heck, yes. The Breaks got discovered by Dan'l Boone, you know. But he turned back, said the goin' was too hard. Some of us like it, though. Tough people for a tough country. I bet you'd like living here, though, if'n you had someone to go home to at night."

"Hey." Jack pointed. "There's a truck pulled off up ahead."

Shadow couldn't see it until he'd taken a few more steps. A white GMC step-van sat overlooking the valley below. Black letters on the rusty hood, written backwards, spelled, "BAILEY'S BOILERS," above a Virginia license plate.

As they neared it, Jack crossed over to join the other two.

"Might be broke down," he said. "But it wasn't here when we drove by earlier."

Shadow walked up, looking at the ground as he did. Someone with large feet, wearing boots, had gotten out and walked over to the guardrail at the edge of the pullover. The prints were indistinct in the gravel, other than the first where, when the man had stepped down, his heel digging in. Shadow followed the prints, with

23

his eyes, to the guardrail.

He looked at the truck. On the side of the cargo compartment was a cartoon of a running mechanic in bib overalls, holding a wrench, along with, "BAILEY'S BOILERS," and a phone number. He looked in the driver side window. The inside was a mess, soda cans, fast food bags and wrappers, rags, tools and other junk all over. Among the trash on the cluttered console sat a stained, Styrofoam coffee cup that had obviously been used as a chewing-tobacco spittoon. An ashtray overflowed. A glance down showed that the floor of the truck was also filthy and the cargo area looked just as cluttered. Both doors were locked.

He walked around to the back of the truck. A large padlock in a crude, hand-installed hasp held the door shut. Someone had had written, "Dirt Test in Progress," in the heavy coating of road grime. He continued on around the truck. No flat tires. He walked over to the guardrail.

"So where's the driver?" Jack asked. "There's nothing back that way for miles. And if he headed for town, we'd have seen him."

Shadow pointed out toward the valley. "He's out there."

"How do you know?"

"Shadder's got eyes like a hawk," said Karen. "He's a heck of a good tracker."

"Oh?" Jack looked down at the gravel. "I don't see anything."

"There's prints." Shadow pointed at the guardrail. "And there's that."

Someone had reached down and grabbed the rail for support as he went over the edge, leaving smudges on the dusty surface. A glance over the rail showed scuffmarks, where the man had gone down a steep trail.

"Now why would someone go down there?" Shadow absentmindedly reached into his pocket for a jellybean. "Plenty of places up here where he could take a leak." He put it in his mouth and sucked on it.

"Maybe he went fishin'," Karen said.

Shadow threw a leg over the guardrail. "Let's go find out."

CHAPTER FOUR

"AIN'T THIS A PUBLIC PARK?"

When they got to the bottom of the drop-off, Shadow found tracks leading south toward Grassy Creek. They hadn't gone a quarter mile when a bear of a man appeared, walking toward them, his shoulder-length black hair matched by a greasy, unkempt beard. He wore faded, stained blue coveralls, the zipper down in front to reveal a torn, filthy tee shirt. In his huge, dirty right hand he carried a satchel, in his other mitt was a folding shovel, probably army surplus. He wore heavy work boots, not very suitable for hiking. On his belt was a holster containing an old-west style revolver, a large caliber weapon judging from the size. Although there were restrictions on carrying firearms in the park, Shadow wasn't quite sure if they were in the park or not, or even which state they were in. Probably not the park, though, because neither of the other rangers seemed upset by the gun.

The man waved and grinned when he saw the three rangers, who stopped and waited as he approached. The wind came from behind him, carrying the smell of some sort of fuel oil mingled with tobacco odors and unwashed human. Shadow saw that the name "Ben" had been embroidered on the coveralls.

"Ho, there," the man said. "Looks like I done found me a ranger convention."

"You might say that," said Shadow. "That your truck up by the highway?"

"Shore is." He turned his head and shot a stream of tobacco juice through the air. "Why? Did I park in a handicapped space? I didn't see no NO PARKING sign."

"We ain't worried about that," Karen said. "We're looking for a lost girl and jes' happened on your truck."

"Shit, I'm fergittin my manners." The big man stooped and set his bag down with the shovel on top. He held out his hand and smiled, revealing a nearly toothless mouth. "I'm Ben Bailey. They calls me Boiler Ben."

When all of them had finished shaking hands and introducing themselves,

Karen asked. "You haven't seen anybody, have you?"

"Nope. Not a soul."

"What are you doing down here, anyway?" Shadow asked.

"You're not from these parts are you?" Bailey shot out another stream of brown juice.

"What's it to you?"

"If you was from around here," Bailey answered, "you'd know it ain't polite to be so nosy. My business is my own."

"You're on park property," said Jack, with an unfriendly edge in his voice. "That makes it our business."

"Ain't this a public park?"

"It is."

"Then I got a right to be here." He spat again. "I'm part of the public. But I'll tell you anyways. I seen what might be a cave down here and figgered I'd take a looky-see. I'm always hopin' to find Swift's treasure."

Jack said, "You saw a cave all the way down here? From the highway?"

"Believe what you want, Buster." Bailey bent and picked up his things. "I ain't got time to chitchat." He grinned widely and walked back toward the highway.

"What a character," Shadow said.

"Seemed like a regular feller to me," said Karen. "I wouldn't want someone to be pokin' their noses into my business, neither."

"I don't like that guy, though." Jack said.

"Why didn't we confiscate his gun, then?" Shadow asked. "You said we're in the park."

"We don't generally do that. There's no signs here on the Kentucky side, so hunters sometimes stray across the border. So we cut them some slack, even that guy."

There was a bitter tone to the remark that made Shadow wonder. "You know him from somewhere?"

"Yep. He did some business with my brother, years ago. He's a scumbag."

*

When the rangers stopped for lunch, sitting on boulders along the creek, Shadow asked, "What was that crack the boiler guy made? About some sort of treasure?"

"You ain't heard about the lost silver mines of John Swift?" Karen rummaged in her lunch bag.

"Never heard of it."

"Seems back in the days before the revolutionary war, a party of Frenchies from the coast came out west and wounded a bear. They followed it to its den in a cave and discovered silver veins right on the surface of the rock. Dug some out and started back east, but the Shawnee killed all but one. Him they kept as a slave."

Shadow swallowed a bite of sandwich. "John Swift?"

"Naw, I said this was a Frenchy." Karen unwrapped a sandwich. "After a few years, he gets loose, but the French-Indian War is going on. After the war, he comes back on an expedition with this John Swift feller and takes him back to the cave. They start mining the silver and sending it east on pack mules."

"And the mine's around here?"

"Naw. Most reckon it was farther west. But they always packed out through here. The Injuns would attack the pack trains and sometimes kill the mules. The miners would bury that mule's load or stash it in a cave."

"Didn't they come back for it?" Shadow asked.

"Naw, as I remember, this Swift feller went to England for some reason and then got—what do they call it, keelhauled, shanghaied?—into the British navy."

"Impressed," Shadow suggested.

Karen blushed. "Aw, it ain't so much. Lots o' folks can tell you the story."

Jack spoke quickly. "Wasn't that during the American Revolution? And they threw him in jail for a while, too."

"Anyway," Karen took a bite and chewed for a moment, "by the time he got hisself free, he was old and blind. Never could find his way back."

"So has anyone ever found any silver?"

"Who knows? If anyone from around here found some, you think he'd tell folks so Uncle Sam could take it away in taxes? That ain't the way we do things in these here parts."

And that ain't the half of it, Shadow thought.

John Bushore

CHAPTER FIVE

"WHERE DID YOU LEARN TO TALK LIKE THAT?"

Ten days later, the futile search for Caitlin Bledsoe had been called off. Shadow, in a suit and tie, sat at a courtroom table with a lawyer, trying to catch his daughter's eye. The judge hadn't come in yet, and the only sound was that of a lawyer shuffling papers.

Shadow had filed for a hearing in Richmond, the state's capitol, since that was where his ex-wife now lived. He had driven clear across the state from Breaks Interstate Park, nearly a nine-hour drive. As he drove across the state, spring seemed more advanced as he traveled east, dropping down in elevation toward the coast.

Ashley was fidgeting, obviously upset. Her mother had put her on the far side, away from Shadow. Once in a while Ashley would begin to look over at her father, but her mother would nudge her.

Looking at Jessica, his ex-wife, Shadow wondered what he'd ever seen in her. She had changed a lot since he'd last seen her, and not for the better in his opinion. Her skin, which had been attractively tanned when he'd first met her at the sweet young age of sixteen—although she'd said she was twenty—was now a pasty white, accentuated by her red raspberry lipstick and violet eye shadow. Her hair was bright blonde with wisps of strawberry coloring and her violet dress reminded him of over-ripe blueberries, the fabric stretched across her chest as though plump fruits were ready to burst. Apparently she'd been able to afford breast augmentation since marrying tort lawyer Wilford Armistead, III, her present husband.

Her new husband wasn't in the courtroom today, which didn't surprise Shadow. Wilford was probably in another court somewhere, suing a drug company or tire manufacturer for millions of dollars on behalf of the "little guy." The way Shadow saw it, Wilford got rich while all those little guys got peanuts.

Instead, a man with Asian features, unknown to Shadow and presumably her lawyer, sat next to Jessica. Probably from the same firm as Armistead, Shadow figured, just like Jessica to save a few bucks where she could get a discount or a freebie.

When Jessica leaned over to ask her attorney something, Ashley gave Shadow a sidelong glance and a quick smile, then looked forward again. She was wearing braces, he noticed. No surprise, Jessica had added his share of the orthodontist's expenses to his monthly bill for child support. He also observed that she wore make-up, something he'd never quite approved of—and she didn't need it anyway. She was a pretty girl with brown wavy hair and soft brown eyes. And a beautiful smile, braces or not.

Knowing she'd look back again, Shadow reached into his shirt pocket for the bag of jellybeans he always carried. Selecting two, he unobtrusively slipped them into his mouth, positioned them with his tongue and bit down on them, one at a time.

Then he faced Ashley and waited.

Sure enough, she looked over again and he opened his mouth in a wide grin, a black jellybean hanging from each upper incisor like a vampire with rotten fangs, a face he'd often made when his daughter was little. Ashley's eyes lit up and she brought her hand to her mouth to smother a fit of laughter.

Jessica took a quick glance at Ashley, then whirled around to glare at Shadow. Instead of trying to cover up what he'd done, Shadow waggled his eyebrows and grinned even more broadly. Just then a door near the front of the courtroom opened and a gray-haired woman in a judge's robe emerged, facing Shadow. Her eyes went wide and her head jerked back in shock.

"All rise," the bailiff announced and chair legs scraped as everyone came to their feet, "for the honorable Judge. . ."

Shadow snapped his mouth shut and scrambled out of his chair. One of the jellybeans became dislodged and somehow got sucked into the back of his throat. He choked and began to cough.

For a moment, he stood bent over, his hand over his mouth. Luckily the candy came loose and popped into his palm. He straightened and looked around. Everyone else had sat back down. He slunk down into his seat, sorry that he'd forgotten himself with the joy of seeing Ashley and acted the fool. In front of the judge, no less.

The thin-faced woman behind the bench put on a pair of glasses and put out a hand to the court clerk sitting beside the bench. The young clerk, with a hand over her mouth as though to hide a smile, gave her a file and the judge began reading. Every once in a while, she would give Shadow a sidelong glance. Shadow noticed that his lawyer, Arthur Ellison, had edged away from him slightly. Ellison, whom Shadow had only met one other time since hiring him, was a heavy-set, pretentious young man, apparently just out of law school. His face was flushed.

Looking over at the other table, he saw that Ashley's face was also red and her head was lowered. Jessica, on the other hand, had her face in her hands and was trembling slightly. Shadow realized she was laughing. He swallowed the remaining jellybean, feeling like the world's biggest idiot. The other jellybean—the one in his hand—he discreetly scraped off on the side of his chair. Having nothing else to get the sticky mess off his palm, he then wiped his hands on his pants.

After what seemed an eternity to Shadow, the judge announced that the hearing was to re-examine the court's earlier ruling concerning Mr. Hubert Fletcher in the matter of his daughter, Ashley Fletcher, which had been determined in the Juvenile and Domestic Court of Virginia Beach, Virginia, on November twenty-third. . .

Shadow hardly listened. All it boiled down to was that, since the divorce, he'd only been allowed visitation rights, which meant he was limited to taking Ashley on day trips and only if he traveled here, to Williamsburg, all the way across the state. He'd seen her just six or seven times in the last two years. By the time she grew up, he'd hardly know her.

He'd let things stand that way out of shame for what he'd been accused of doing—and not wanting to put Ashley through another court battle—but he had finally decided to fight back. It wasn't fair that he should be denied spending time with his daughter for something he hadn't done.

Suddenly he realized his attorney was coming to his feet. Shadow rose also.

"Your Honor," Ellison said, "My client petitions the court to set aside the earlier ruling, concerning custody, in this matter. That decision was based on an allegation, which Mr. Fletcher denies, that he inappropriately touched his daughter on one, and only one, instance. We ask that Mr. Fletcher be allowed six weekend-long visits and two full weeks a year with custody of his daughter."

"Thank you, Mr. Ellison," the judge said.

Ellison sat and Shadow followed.

The judge—Shadow hadn't caught her name and hoped it wouldn't matter—turned toward those seated at the other table, saying, "And what is your client's position, Mr. Takenata?"

The lawyer, along with Jessica, stood.

Takenata cleared his throat. "My client's position has not changed since the earlier decision, Your Honor. She feels her daughter might be at risk if Mr. Fletcher is granted increased custody rights, especially since she would be staying alone in the same home with the. . ." He glanced over at Shadow as though he'd been about to say something different, and then finished his sentence. "with Mr. Fletcher."

"Thank you, Mr. Takenata." The judge looked down at her papers. "I've familiarized myself with the earlier decision. Mr. Fletcher?"

Shadow rose. "Yes, Your Honor?"

She lowered her head and looked at him over her glasses, with the corners of her lips turned down. "Do you have any new evidence to present?"

"No, Your Honor."

"Then what do you base your request upon?"

"Nothing, Your Honor. That is to say, nothing has changed. But I kept quiet, before because I didn't want to put Ashley through any more. She'd already been through plenty in the divorce. But I never touched her in any way that a father shouldn't touch his daughter and I've realized how much I've missed her. Just because her mother and I can't get along, that doesn't mean I shouldn't be with her."

The judge glared at him. "This has nothing to do with you and your ex-wife getting along, Mr. Fletcher. What concerns the court is that you could have disputed the earlier decision, yet you did not. That would have been the proper time to ask for visitation rights."

"Yes, Your Honor." His heart sank, even though Ellison had warned him this might be the court's position.

"I see also that you're a combat-wounded, decorated veteran."

"Yes, ma'am."

"Well," continued the judge, "since you have virtually no visitation rights at all and are not asking for joint custody, I see no reason not to re-open the issue." She shuffled her papers. "Do you live alone, Mr. Fletcher?"

"Yes, ma'am."

"I understand you're a park ranger and live in a remote area?"

"Well, yes, Your Honor, I'm a ranger. And I live in the park, but near the other rangers and their families. It's almost like a little neighborhood."

"And how large is your home?"

"It's small," he admitted. "But there are two bedrooms." Then, trying to think of something positive to say, added, "And it's in a beautiful wooded area and the park has a restaurant, a lake and trails, even a swimming pool. It would be like Ashley taking a vacation when she visited. And it wouldn't take away from her schooling; it could be in the late spring or summer when it's really beautiful in the mountains."

"I'm sure," the judge said dryly. She looked around at the courtroom. "My greatest concern," she said, "is this allegation of fondling. Since there is no physical evidence or witnesses other than the parties concerned, I'm going to have Child Protective Services conduct individual interviews of all family members with an eye to the child's safety. Also, I want Mr. Fletcher's living arrangements looked at, since he lives in a rather unusual location." She looked toward Shadow with a wry smile.

Shadow wondered if that was good or bad. At least it seemed better than the earlier baleful looks.

"Unless there are any objections," the judge continued, "I'm going to continue this case for two months."

Jessica's lawyer immediately rose. "Your Honor, this was all settled in the earlier hearing. Re-opening this issue would bring up old memories harmful to the child. She's been in counseling as it is."

"Counseling?" The judge raised an eyebrow. "And is this counseling deemed necessary to the, um, allegations of improper touching?"

Takenata hesitated. "Well, not specifically. But the divorce has caused her some emotional problems."

"I'm sure it has." She took off her reading glasses. "Divorce is unsettling to all concerned. But the counseling isn't due to the allegation, so I find that irrelevant."

Takenata nodded and sat.

She turned toward Shadow's table. "Is that satisfactory to the petitioner?"

"That would be agreeable, Your Honor."

Putting her glasses back on, the judge looked down at the papers, avoiding looking into anyone's eyes. "The law is quite clear that the state must look into the circumstances before allowing any modification of custody agreements. So this case will be continued, pending completion of the earlier stipulations until. . ." She turned to the clerk sitting next to her.

The clerk scheduled another court session three months down the road. And then it was over and everyone was leaving the courtroom. Although his lawyer had warned him not to expect too much, too fast, Shadow sat, disappointed. He'd hoped to spend at least some time with her this summer.

Ellison's voice broke his reverie. "Well, Mr. Fletcher, I'll see you in two months."

Shadow nodded and shook the lawyer's hand. He made his way out of the courtroom and, to his surprise, came upon Ashley sitting on a bench in the small corridor. Jessica was nowhere to be seen.

"Hello, Sweetheart," he said. "It's so good to see you."

She jumped up and gave him a hug. "I've missed you, Dad."

He kissed her cheek. "We're going to fix that, though, aren't we. It may take a while, but it'll happen."

"We've only got a minute," she said, glancing toward the exit door. "I told Mom I had to use the restroom."

Shadow nodded. "How have you been?"

"Okay, I guess." She still held him about the waist. "I'm getting used to the new school and all, but I can't stand Wilford; he's a pompous ass."

"Ashley," he said. "I can't believe you'd talk that way."

She stepped back and looked up at him, tears forming in the corners of her eyes. "Well, he is. And he's always taking Mom out to dinner or somewhere and they go away for weekends and I'm stuck in that big, old house, all alone. We're way out in the country, so I can't even ask friends over."

"They leave you alone?"

"No, they always hire this woman to come be with me. But she watches TV all day and probably wouldn't know if I died up in my room." Ashley wiped her eyes furiously.

"But isn't it nice living like that in a big house with all those fancy things?"

"It sucks."

"Ashley!"

Ashley's face went livid with anger. "I don't know why they got married anyway. Wilford is a jerk—just a jerk with money—and I don't know what he sees in Mom. She's just spending his money. Maybe she gives good blowjobs."

Shadow, stunned, didn't know what to say. This was his little girl; she was only twelve and she talked like a tramp. He hadn't even known what a blowjob was at that age.

Finally, he shook his head. "Ashley, I don't know what's come over you. Where did you learn to talk like that?"

"I hear things," she said defiantly, "when they don't notice I'm around." Then she burst into tears. "I have to go." She hugged him again. "I love you, Daddy."

She let go and ran out the door.

CHAPTER SIX

"AND THIS WILL PROTECT ME?"

Shadow drove out of Richmond in his private vehicle, an older model Dodge compact, going northeast on State Highway 30, rather than west toward The Breaks. Since he was in this part of the country, he'd decided to see if he could learn more about his latest encounter with evil. He knew that his own spirit had made some connection to Native American spiritualism, but why did it feel different this time? And he certainly didn't feel it now, away from the mountains.

He traveled through a quiet countryside of farms and horse pastures until, at a town with the unusual name of Central Garage, he turned of on State Road 30, now heading southeast. After the town of King William, he cut due south on a county road, 633. This poorly maintained country lane, he knew, ended up at the twelve-hundred-acre Pamunkey Indian Reservation along the river. This small piece of land and the even smaller holding of the Mattaponi Reservation on the nearby Mattaponi River, made up the sum total of all that was left of the territory of the Powhatan Confederation, owing their existence to treaties made in the mid-1600's. He passed mostly woods now, with an occasional run-down house, trailer, or double-wide on a brick foundation. Dirt roads ran into the woods, undoubtedly leading to the homes of those living a bit farther from the road.

He turned left just before reaching the reservation and bounced over the ruts and potholes, turning off the road onto one of the dirt paths. A couple of hundred yards farther, invisible from the road, sat an old frame home, tanned paint faded and peeling. A huge pile of neatly stacked firewood nearly filled the porch. The front yard showed neat and mowed but, at the back of the house, wilderness began. But not a pristine wood, for through the underbrush could be seen an old, rusty bicycle frame, assorted appliances, tires and debris, even the dilapidated remains of an old pick up truck.

He hit the brakes with a cloud of dust, honked the horn to announce himself and got out. As he walked up to the porch, no one showed to greet him and he wondered if anyone was home, but then heard earnest voices coming through the window screen, a man and a woman arguing. He smiled.

Opening the door, he stuck in his head and peered into the relatively dark interior. The smell of fried fish, the staple food of the native riverfolk for centuries, permeated the air. The floral perfume of air freshener mixed with the cooking smell without masking it. By the far wall, a TV stood on a wheeled stand, revealing the arguing couple he'd heard. Between Shadow and the screen stood the back of a large chair. From here, no one could be seen.

"What's this?" he asked. "Too addicted to the soaps to greet your long-lost grandson?"

"You've not been gone that long," a sharp, high voice came from the chair. "And, if you don't let me see if Genevieve leaves the cheap son-of-a-bitch this time, I'll disown you as my grandson."

"I love you, too, Grandma Min."

"Get in here and close the door; you're letting the flies in. And hush up."

He did as she asked and stood looking around the room. It hadn't changed that much since he'd last seen it. In fact, it hadn't changed much since he was a kid. Except maybe the pictures hung on the wall. The current president's portrait hung in the presidential place of honor, as had every president before him, although William Jefferson Clinton's portrait had been turned toward the wall following his sexual transgressions. Besides the chair out in the center, there was a matching green sofa along the right wall; a well-used fireplace graced the left. The usual side tables, lamps and fixtures of a 1960's era home filled most of the rest of the space. On the table to Grandma Min's right, alongside the TV remote, rested a signed photograph of Former-Senator Hubert H. Humphrey, one of her prized possessions. She had met the politician at a fund-raiser in Richmond many years ago, and considered him one of the smartest men to ever be elected, even if it wasn't in her own state.

Shadow went over and sat on the edge of the sofa, noticing a cloud of dust arise as he settled. When he was growing up, the house had always been immaculate, but he doubted Grandma Min could even see the dust.

She sat back in the chair, a thin, small woman in an old, flowery housecoat, with her cloudy eyes fixed on the TV screen from behind her old-fashioned glasses. Her face was brown and heavily wrinkled, as was befitting an old woman, but her coifed hair showed shiny black. Unless you looked at the roots, another thing that was probably beyond her notice. Fuzzy pink slippers adorned her feet atop the ottoman that matched neither the chair nor the sofa.

Luckily for Shadow, he'd come in at the end of the soap. The characters faded out and Grandma Min snatched up the remote, turning off the TV as it announced, "Will Genevieve take Samuel back? Tune in tomor. . ."

She turned her gaze to Shadow. "Well, look what the cat dragged in. An ungrateful wretch, too busy to drop in on his ol' granny now and then."

He snorted. "You just said I haven't been away that long."

"Don't contradict your elders," she snapped. "Well, get over here and give me a kiss, at least."

He got up, bent over, and pecked her on the cheek while her bony arms encircled him. She smelled of talcum powder and—what else?—fried fish.

"Hmm, hmm," she hummed in appreciation. "Hubert, you're a sight for sore eyes.

"You, too, Grandma Min. How have you been doing?" He went back to the sofa.

"Well as can be expected. So what brings you up here from waaay down in Virginia Beach, only a couple hours drive keeping you from visiting me?"

"Actually I'm not working there any longer. I've been transferred to another park, clear across the state."

"That's not what I asked," she said. "I asked what brought you here. I can see you've got something on your mind. Would you like a beer?"

"Beer would be nice."

"In the fridge. Get one for me, too, while you're up."

Shadow went to the kitchen and pulled two beers from the old fashioned refrigerator. Taking two glasses from a cupboard—Grandma Min thought drinking from a can to be uncouth—he filled them both and carried them out. He grabbed a couple of coasters from a rack on the coffee table and set down brews for each of them.

Grandma Min said, "So? Out with it."

He took a long pull on his beer, grateful for the cool liquid after his day in court. "Well. . .," he said, "I guess I *have* been staying away. There was some trouble down at the park in Virginia Beach and, it's a long story, but the thing that bothered me is that I could feel an evil spirit, if you know what I mean by feel, and it sort of creeped me out. I didn't know if I should tell you about it."

Grandma Min picked up her glass and considered it, as though consulting a crystal ball. "What kind of spirit?"

"A wolfwraith, at least that's what I think of it as. It possessed an old man and there were killings. I ended up fighting the thing."

"You went up against it? And you survived?" She raised her eyebrows and sipped her beer with a slurping noise.

"You seem surprised."

"Darn straight I am. As far as spirit-things go, you're unarmed." She took the glass to her lips and slurped.

Shadow sighed. What do you mean by that?"Other people might have asked questions about the details, but conversations with Grandma Min seldom followed a logical route. "

"Hubert, I warned you time and time again over the years. But, nooo, you were all wrapped up in that soldiering mumbo-jumbo. Only reason you never came up against any spirits before now is that you've been on concrete sidewalks in towns or military bases, or overseas somewhere." She slurped more beer. "Now that you're back home, got your feet down on ancestral soil, you'll be troubled by spirits."

"Warned me? About what? I don't remember any warnings."

She grinned. "I kept reminding you, whenever you came home, that you should be wearing the medicine pouch I made for you before you went away."

He laughed, but regretted it when she gave him a sharp look. He took a sip of beer to recover. "Um, sorry, Grandma Min. But, um, I sort of lost that years ago."

She turned her eyes heavenward as though begging to know why she was saddled with such a careless grandson. "And now," she said, "you show up here asking me what to do. But why bother? You got away from the wolf spirit, didn't you?"

"Yes, but now there's been another thing." He shrugged. "I didn't worry about the first one, the wolf-spirit, so much because it was about the same as I'd felt when I lived here with you and Grandfather. But now I've come up against something that seems wrong to me."

"Wrong how?"

He grimaced. "Hard to describe. Evil, malevolent like any bad spirit, yet with an icy, impersonal edge. It didn't seem to be after me, particularly, but I still got a feeling like I was out in the open, absolutely nothing around me but a vast, white plain with nowhere to hide."

Grandma Min set her beer down and began to struggle up out of the chair. "Lie back on the sofa and close your eyes," she said.

"Why?"

"Just do it."

He noticed her walking around behind him as he shut his eyes. Moments later, he felt her bony fingers, still cold from holding the frosty glass, envelop his skull like a clutching spider.

"I want you to remember what you felt," she said. "Try to put yourself back in that moment when you first experienced this new thing."

He began to say that he couldn't remember exactly, but then he was back up on the mountainside, looking into a grotto. Time seemed to stand still, a snapshot of one instant of his life.

"Okay, that did it," said a cracked voice off in the distance.

He opened his eyes and saw Grandma Min sitting back on her chair, considering him. "Where'd this happen?" she asked.

"There was this missing girl and everyone else thought she'd gone lost, but I. . ."

"I know all that. You said this park is clear across the state. Whose land was it, before the Europeans invaded? Shawnee? Cherokee?"

"It was. . ."

"Never mind," Grandma Min waved his answer away before he could finish. "That's all in the past. The main thing is that whatever you felt isn't from around here."

Why'd she ask then? Shadow wondered. "Where from, then?"

"It's from the north."

38

"Iroquois?"

She nodded as though she had a secret. "Much farther."

"Where?"

"How the hell would I know?" She sprang from the chair, suddenly seeming much younger. "I'll make you a good dinner. You should have called and told me you were coming. You could have picked up some groceries."

"How? You don't have a phone."

"I do now." She pulled a cell phone from somewhere on her person. "They sell these little things at a store in town. No wires. You should get one of these."

"Why?" he asked.

"You could be in my calling circle. Maybe you'd bother keeping in touch with your old grandma, then."

*

The next morning, as they said goodbye in front of the house, Grandma Min pulled out a small bag on a leather thong and held it out to him. "Put this on."

He took it and held it in his palm for inspection. "You made me a new protection."

"I put in something from the north, since that seems to be what sort of thing you are up against."

"I'm not up against anything," he said.

She nodded somberly. "You will be."

"And this will protect me?"

Chuckling, she said, "Hell, no. Nothing can protect you from <u>this</u> spirit, who cannot die."

"Then why bother?"

"It will let you talk to the spirit."

"And what good will that do."

She shrugged. "It couldn't hurt. It's like a cell phone—the old fashioned kind."

"What's in it?"

"That's none of your business," said Grandma Min. "Never look inside."

Shadow put it around his neck and tucked it inside his shirt. He would wear this one, he decided. The earlier one would have been no protection against suicide bombers or bullets, but he was facing a different enemy now."But what could you have from the north?" he asked. "You've never left the state."

She grinned. "A duck feather. John Fox from the reservation shot a pintail and gave it to me last year."

He sighed in exasperation. "And that's from the north?"

Grandma Min shook her head in exasperation. "Where do you *think* they go in the summer, Hubert?".

John Bushore

CHAPTER SEVEN

"WEREN'T YOU MISSING A HAND A MINUTE AGO?"

Shadow arrived home in the late afternoon to find that true spring had finally arrived in the mountains. The breezes blew warm from the south, driving the cold northward—where it belonged. And it seemed as though they'd blown away that supernatural atmosphere away as well; he felt not a hint of it.

He was washing up at the sink, naked to the waist, when a knock sounded at the front door. He turned off the water and dried his face with a towel. He put Grandma Min's amulet around his neck and slipped a shirt on as he went through the bedroom, he didn't pick up The Claw, which he'd tossed on a chair. No need for it, just to answer the door.

As he walked, buttoning his shirt one-handed, he saw a blonde woman on the porch. Mrs. Bledsoe. What in the world was she doing here? He opened the door. She wore jeans, a light sweater, and hiking shoes. She'd changed her hairstyle and she looked even better than he'd remembered, with short hair curling up just below the ears.

"Mrs. Bledsoe, good to see you again." He held the door wide. "Come in out of the heat."

"Thank you." She smiled and stepped past him. "But I'm Alexandria Hutton, Cleo's sister. You're Ranger Fletcher?"

"Uh, yes. Sorry, but you. . ."

"Look just like my sister? Well, would twins explain it?"

"Yeah. Yeah, sure."

"I wanted to ask you a few questions about my niece's disappearance. Do you mind?"

He realized he still stood in the doorway. Pulling the door closed, he said, "Of course not. Would you like to sit down?"

"That would be nice, thanks."

"Kitchen table all right?" There were clothes and junk strewn all over the furniture in the living room. He never used it.

She followed him to the kitchen as he finished buttoning his shirt—one-handed of course. He took a dirty coffee cup and spoon off the table and shoved some magazines and a roll of paper towels aside. He pulled out a chair. "Would you like something to drink?"

As she went to sit, he noticed her glance around the room at the dishes in the sink and the clutter on the counters and cabinet tops. Not to mention the overflowing trashcan in the corner, flanked by a leaning broom with straws curved from standing there for most of its life.

"Sorry, maid's day off," he said. "But the health department hasn't shut us down yet."

"Not a problem. Yes, I'll have ice water, please."

He got a glass from a cabinet. Opening the freezer door, he saw that he'd not emptied the ice cube trays. Damn. He couldn't just reach in and grab some cubes from the bin, which was empty. He grabbed one of the plastic trays and set one end on the counter, pinning it down with his left wrist and twisted. A couple of cubes popped out, skittering across the countertop. Without The Claw he had no easy way to get the cubes out. Nothing left to do but to turn the tray over and dump it out. Now all the cubes lie on the counter, except for a couple that had fallen into the sink. He put down the empty tray and, feeling clumsy as all get out, picked a few up and put them in the glass, then swept the remainder into the sink. He picked up the glass, set it on the sink bottom and then turned the tap to fill it, all the while wishing he'd taken a few seconds to put The Claw on. He could feel her watching eyes.

Taking the glass to the table, he set it before her, realizing he should have put a napkin under it; the table wasn't all too clean, either. But he didn't have napkins. He reached out, grabbed the roll of paper towels and put it under his left forearm. Clumsily, he ripped off a towel and set it next to the glass, sort of half-folding it as he did.

"There you go," he said.

She smelled of sweat and bug spray. Damn, she was good-looking. Same blonde hair and blue eyes as her sister, of course, but she somehow seemed prettier. Maybe because he saw that she didn't have a wedding ring on her hand when she reached for the glass?

"Thank you," she replied.

"Uh, look. I was just washing up. Let me finish getting dressed and I'll be right back."

"Sure. No hurry."

Once in the bedroom, he unbuttoned the cuff, pulled up his left shirtsleeve—he didn't own any short-sleeved shirts—and slipped his wrist into The Claw's harness. He hooked the finger-like nub that the surgeons had fashioned under The

Claw's lever and then tightened the Velcro straps with his real hand. He pulled the sleeve down and buttoned the cuff.

Going into the bathroom, he quickly brushed his teeth, which is what he'd been about to do when interrupted. He grabbed a brush and ran it through his short hair. Should he shave? No, she'd already seen his stubble and would think he was trying to impress her, maybe.

And then he stopped abruptly and looked his reflection in the eye. "You dumb shit," he murmured. This woman had come about her missing niece. He needed to get real.

Returning to the kitchen, he pulled out a chair and sat next to her, crossing his forearms on the table. "Sorry about that."

"Not a problem." She stared at The Claw.

"What would you like to ask me?"

She looked at the right hand, then raised her eyes to his. "I, um, wanted to know if you. . . if Caitlin, um. . . Can I ask you something else first?"

"Not a problem," he mimicked.

"Did. . . weren't you missing a hand a minute ago?"

He held up The Claw. "You mean this?"

She nodded.

He pulled the cable inside the harness. All four fingers curled in unison until they touched an immobile thumb. The movement looked totally unnatural. "Special effects."

She stared. "That is amazing. It looks completely. . . well, lifelike, until it moves."

Shadow held up his hand beside The Claw. "I was serious when I said special effects. A guy that used to work for the movie studios—you know, making lifelike masks and monster heads and stuff like that—did it up to match my other hand. It's all plastic, covered with foam, then latex skin."

"I didn't know they could do something like that."

"It's fairly new technology. But, war being the way it is now, everybody wears body armor." He lowered his hands back down. "When you get hit, you're more likely to survive, even if you lose a few parts. The Hollywood guys make it look real, and there's a polyethylene string that pulls inside the fingers to curl them at the joints. The thumb doesn't move by itself, but I can position it with my right hand."

"You were in the military?" She looked directly at him, now. He looked into eyes a darker shade of blue than his own.

"Marines."

"And your hand?"

"I played with a firecracker." She blinked in surprise. He regretted what he'd said, then, but enough about the damn claw, he'd have never let her see him without it if he'd had his druthers, as Grandma Min always said. "What can I do for you, Miz. . . I'm sorry, what was it?"

"Hutton. But, after me asking all those personal questions, please just call me

Xan."

"Jan?"

"No, Xan."

"With a 'Z'?"

She grinned. "No, with an 'X'." Short for Al-_ex_-andria."

"Oh, I get it," he said.

"Everybody called me Zan or Zandra when I was growing up. I decided to spell it with an "X." It seemed more exotic." She raised an eyebrow. "And yours?"

"My what?"

"Your first name."

"Oh. I'm Shadow."

"Shadow? That's an unusual name."

He shrugged "If they call you Zan with an 'X', then my name can be Shadow."

She looked him up and down and grinned. "Hmm. Tall, dark and handsome and mysterious, too. You intrigue me, Shadow."

He gulped. "My grandmother named me that, sort of."

"Sort of?"

"Well, I'm mostly Native American and. . ."

"Mm-hmm," she hummed as though in appreciation.

"Grandma Min claims to be the only surviving Accomattoc Indian—except me, she says I'm one too—but I don't buy into that so much. She's got this thing. Sort of like, 'the South will rise again,' that they say here in Virginia but with her it's the tribes that are going to come out on top."

"And so?"

Why was he telling her all this? But, deep down, he knew. He wanted to keep her here as long as he could and he'd talk as long as she acted interested. Had she really called him handsome? "Well, she sort of named me 'Avenging Shadow.'"

Her grin never faltered. "You're kidding."

"And that's not the worst of it."

"This I've got to hear."

"Grandma Min was a big fan of Hubert Humphrey." Shadow took a deep breath. "My full name is Hubert Avenging Shadow Fletcher."

For a moment, he thought she'd laugh, but she recovered. "Fletcher? That's not an Indian name."

"I'm not all Indian. There's probably not any 'full-blood' Indians in Virginia after all these years of 'white occupation,' as Grandma Min calls it. Fletcher is Scottish."

"How unusual." She'd stopped grinning now and she looked interested.

"Back when the Europeans first came, the Native American women wanted to have fair-skinned children, so they'd be treated as whites. They had no idea it wouldn't make any difference, so long as their kids had any Indian blood. Anyway, they married—or mated with—the fairest of men. Since so many Scottish men were exiled here by the English, there was a surplus of single Scottish men to be had."

"But didn't they realize that the whites wouldn't. . . Oh, listen to me. I came to ask you about my niece and all I do is pry into your ancestry. I'm sorry."

"Don't be. I don't mind. But what did you want to ask me?"

Her smile faded and the sparkle left her eyes. "They—some rangers I talked to—they said you thought Caitlin might have been. . . abducted?"

"It looked that way to me."

"In what way?"

Shadow stood abruptly. "Would you like a beer?"

"No thanks, just the water."

He got a beer, popped the top and returned to the table.

"Let me think how to put this." He took a swallow of beer and contemplated. "Sometimes I just feel things. It looked like somebody had been lurking near the trail. And then I found a piece of your niece's bracelet. I know that doesn't add up to much, but. . ."

"But," she echoed, "you don't have any proof, just an intuition basically."

"My intuitions are usually pretty good."

She smiled wistfully. "Even so, I've got to believe that she's okay, that there's still a chance of finding her."

"I understand," he said. "I'd do the same."

"They've called off the search for her, you know."

"Yeah, I know."

She took a sip of water and sighed. "I can't have children."

"What?" He wondered what that had to do with anything.

"I was married for a while." She smiled sadly. "And I found out I can never have children. Caitlin is my godchild and—deep in my heart—I've always pretended she was my own daughter." She picked up the paper towel in her left hand and dabbed at her eyes. "I can't stop searching."

Shadow reached out and touched her hand. "Would you like some help?"

John Bushore

CHAPTER EIGHT

"AND THAT'S AN OLD SHAWNEE LEGEND?"

"Good-lookin', huh? " Jack said shuffled the deck for another game.

"You saw the missing girl's mother, didn't you? " Shadow said from the refrigerator as he reached in for a beer. "This one's her twin. "

Jack whistled. "That's good-lookin' all right. No wonder you're going to help her search. "

"It's not that, Jack. " He put the bottle between his left forearm and his body and screwed off the cap with his hand. "Well, maybe, but it's not just that. She seems like a great person and I can understand how she feels. I've got a daughter of my own, remember? " He threw the cap toward the garbage can, but missed. It went behind the can, though, so he didn't worry about it.

Jack set the deck on the table and looked up. "Not married, either, is she? "

Shadow pulled out a chair and sat. "Screw you. I'd help her even if she was. "

"She got a boyfriend? "

"Deal the cards. "

"Do you think there's still any chance of finding that girl? Way I remember it, you said she was maybe taken to the highway, so she was probably taken far from here. "

"But I don't *know* that. " Shadow swigged his beer. "I'm mostly just going by a feeling, I guess. "

Jack shoved the cards toward him. "Cut. Are you even sure it *was* a footprint? "

"Of course. It was a heel impression and the son of a bitch had feet maybe even bigger than yours." Shadow cut the deck.

"Maybe it was Bigfoot then." He picked up his glass and took a long drink. "If it was all that big."

"Get serious. There must be some explanation besides imaginary ape-men for

47

what happened to that kid. She didn't just get lost."

Jack picked up the cards and began to deal. "You're the only one who thinks that. Just forget it, will you?"

"I'm not going to forget it. But Caitlin's aunt is going to keep looking for her and I'm going to help her starting tomorrow." He took a drink. "And you're not being any help at all. Bigfoot, my ass."

"But you still haven't figured out why a man would take a child from a place like that, when he had no way to get her away. So maybe whatever took her didn't need to get to a road. And there's not many men with feet bigger than mine. So you're looking for a giant or a baby Bigfoot, take your pick." Jack set the deck down and picked up his hand. "Or maybe a Yeahoh," he said with an ominous tone.

"Oh, I get it now. You've got another of the old stories to tell me and this is your way of leading up to it." Shadow looked at his cards, discarded two. "Okay, I'll bite. What the hell is a 'Yeahoh'?"

Jack took a drink, then poured in a generous slug of whiskey, adding coke from a can. "You ain't never heard of it?"

"No, but I'm sure I'm about to." Shadow laid down his unplayed hand with a sigh. Card playing was over. When the Shawnee got in this mood, he became talkative and lost interest in the game. Shadow wondered sometimes if it was because Jack's vision got too blurred with alcohol to read the cards.

Sure enough, Jack leaned his chair back on its rear legs and clutched the drink glass to his chest, showing no interest in the game they'd been about to play.

"Seems this man was out huntin' on Pine Mountain. He got lost and a blizzard come up. He come to a big hole in the ground and he thought he would ride out the storm inside. Well, there was this female creature down there, like a cross between a human and a hairy bear and it had deer meat hangin' up and other foods piled around the walls. The man was afraid at first and kept his distance, but the creature didn't bother him. This man hadn't eaten in a long time, so he went over and cut off some deer meat with his knife and still the thing just watched him, like it was wondering what the man might be.

"The man wasn't about to eat the deer meat raw, so he took out his flint and made a fire. He roasted the meat on a stick and started eating it. The hairy creature acted like it wanted a piece, so the man give her some. It took a taste, smacked its lips, and commenced to eatin' it up, saying 'Yeahoh, Yeahoh.'" Jack swallowed half his drink in two gulps and belched.

"Well, the man lived there with it a long time," he went on, "and they got along all right. Then, after a bit, there was a young'un born to 'em. . ."

"Sounds like they got along all right," Shadow said.

"Not all that much. Seems the Yeahoh took such a liking to the man, it wouldn't let him leave. He tried to slip away several times, but she always chased him down and brought him back. Anyway, their baby was half-man, half Yeahoh. But finally, the man was walking along the shore and he found a boat. He got on it and sailed out. Well, the Yeahoh followed him to the shore and commenced to wailin'. She ripped their baby in half and threw the parts after him. And the man just sailed away." Jack drank the other half of his drink and looked at Shadow expectantly.

"Uh. . . is that the end?"

"What did you expect?"

"Well, some kind of logic maybe." Shadow tossed his can into the nearby trashcan and wondered if he could handle another. "Where the hell did the 'shore' come from? And the boat? Pine Mountain is nowhere near the ocean." In fact, the park was located on one of the peaks of Pine Mountain, which was almost 150 miles across.

"You're not supposed to understand it. You're just supposed to listen to it." Jack belched again. "I can't tell that one to the schoolchildren, you know. I don't get to tell it much."

"And that's an old Shawnee legend?"

Jack shrugged. "Actually, I think it could be something the whites started. Who knows?"

"The whites? Where'd you come up with that idea?"

"Daniel Boone bragged that he killed a ten-foot hairy creature with his rifle." Jack took a hit straight from the bottle. "And he called it a 'Yahoo.'" He stood up. "Ponder that, my friend." He went out the door, bottle in hand, without the least bit of a stagger in his walk.

Despite the late hour, Shadow decided he was up for one more. He lurched out of his chair, fetched another beer and went out on the porch. The air was bitterly cold but it felt good after the stuffy kitchen. He sat on the porch rail and studied the tapestry of stars above him, magnificent from his lofty view atop a mountain peak.

Thinking back on Jack's story, he remembered that Jack had said the Yeahoh would not let the man leave. He thought of Karen McCoy.

She'd been nagging him with personal questions ever since the day Caitlin Bledsoe had disappeared. He'd usually managed to keep from telling too much, especially now that he knew she was active in church affairs. Religion didn't interest Shadow; he'd had enough of being ordered around while in the navy. The last thing he needed was some preacher telling him how to live his private life.

Then, all his suspicions about Karen's intentions had come to a head just before he'd left for the custody hearing. "I know your regular days off are Tuesday and Wednesday," she had said. "And I just thought I'd mention that we're having a barbecue at our church a week from Wednesday. Since you're not from the area and don't have any kin in these parts, I thought you might like to get to know some folks."

"I'm sorry, Karen," he'd said. "I'd be delighted to meet some local people, but I promised Jack I'd go looking for artifacts that day."

"Oh, him." Karen was obviously disappointed. "He's a heathen, you know."

"Jack's not so bad," he said, wishing he could think of some better defense of his card-playing buddy. "He's still single, that's all. Sowing his oats, I guess."

"Well, you're single, ain't you? I don't see you out chasin' women." She stepped closer and smiled like a cat that had just found a bird with a broken wing. "You seem like the type who needs to settle down with a good woman, Shadder."

"Um, well, no. I'm, uh, not over my divorce yet, I guess." He went to a cabinet and made a pretense of looking for a file. "I guess I need some time to sort out my life before I get involved again."

But now that he'd met Xan Hutton, maybe he *would* start "chasin' women.

CHAPTER NINE

"YOU'RE AMAZING, DID YOU KNOW THAT?"

Shadow followed Xan up a fissure between two towering rocks, admiring the view. They'd been on the mountain for nearly three hours now, climbing near the northeastern corner of the park, on the Kentucky side, and hardly a word had passed. The sun had come to their side of the hills and the day had begun to warm. Shadow wiped sweat from his face and wondered when and if she was ever going to take a break. He still hadn't entirely adjusted to the thin air of the mountains.

It had been three days since he'd offered to help her search, and this was his first day off work. Xan had met him down along the highway, dressed in jeans, tee shirt and a floppy hat that hid her short, blonde hair. She wore hiking boots and a lightweight backpack.

The fissure opened out at the top and they emerged at the base of a tall, jagged, overhanging cliff, where part of the mountain had broken away. Most of the debris had gone farther down the mountain. They'd climbed over it, but there were plenty of other rock fragments strewn at the base of the cliff.

"Whew, " he said, gesturing at a waist-high ledge nearby. "Let's sit for a moment. "

"Suits me. " She wiped her brow and he noticed sweat stains beneath her arms. "It's beginning to get hot. "

He went and sat on the ledge, taking off his pack. She stood looking out over the land below.

"God, this is beautiful country. "

"I guess so. " Shadow rummaged in his bag. "I sort of prefer the coast, sunrise over the ocean, smell of the sea. " He pulled out a candy bar. "But that's

51

just what I'm used to. I've been all over the world and there's good and bad in every place. Would you like a trail bar or some candy? "

"No, thanks. " She came over and sat a couple of feet from him, taking a water bottle from a side pocket of her pack. "We probably need to break for lunch soon, anyway. "

"Why'd you choose this area? " He tore open the wrapper. "I doubt your niece would climb way up here. "

She paused with the water halfway to her lips. "I don't know. All I can do is search one area at a time and I hadn't been here yet. " She shrugged. "And maybe we'll see something down below."

"Pretty good view from up here. You might be right. "

Below them lay a rugged, uneven valley, with patches of green trees interspersed with rocky areas. The highway and the river showed through in several places. Across the way rose several peaks and, beyond that, massive ridges rolled away into the distance like waves on a green sea, the highest peaks rising like islands. Shadow felt exposed to the view of the gods above, as though something powerful and magnificent judged him from the heavens.

Xan put her water bottle away. "Well, if you'll excuse me for a moment, I need to look behind those rocks over there for the little girl's room. Too much coffee this morning, I guess. " She took off her pack and set it down.

"Sure, I'll just sit and enjoy the view. "

The rocks she'd mentioned were a little ways off. He watched her make her way over the rugged ground, again admiring the way she moved. Not that she tried to look sexy; she didn't have to try. She had a certain grace about her, a self-confident way of carrying herself.

When she'd gone out of sight, he noticed a foot long hunk of wood, nearly three inches thick, probably fallen from the trees up near the peak. The rough bark marked it as pine and it was forked on one end.

He finished his candy, then walked over, picked up the stick and examined it. The fork, at the smaller end, had an interesting shape, reminding him of an eagle's wings as it stooped down on prey. He reached for his boatswain's knife in the leather case attached to his belt. Snapping it open and began to whittle off the fork, since he didn't want to carry the whole branch.

The knife felt good in his hand; he'd used if for so many years that its blade had thinned considerably from years of sharpening. He'd bought it from the ship's store that time he'd been stationed on a navy cruiser as part of the marine guard. A friendly boatswain's mate had taught him about knots and rigging. A boatswain's knife differed from other knives by having a spike—a marlinspike, it was called—that swung out from the opposite side of the blade. This was a four inch, round shaft of metal with a point, used for slipping in between the weaves of a rope line to separate them. There was also a contrivance that would look much like a distorted can opener to a landlubber's eye, a shackle-releasing tool.

Shadow had been whittling as long as he could remember, especially during those military days of "hurry up and wait." He had trouble with carving now, with only one good hand but he kept it up. For one thing, it really helped him develop coordination in his right hand.

Once he'd cut off the excess wood, he adjusted his prosthetic thumb and put the fork in The Claw. With his real hand, he ran the knife's point over the surface of the wood, not cutting yet, just getting the feel for what he'd be able to do. Soon he was in a detached reverie, absorbing the eagle's spirit within the wood. Although he'd carved many animals over the years, he'd never done an eagle. Perhaps now he'd been inspired because several pairs of golden eagles nested in the area.

"Hey, Shadow. Come over here; I found something."

Shadow looked and saw Xan waving from the base of a large boulder, halfway back from where she'd disappeared. He waved and stood to show he'd heard. Putting his knife away, he stuck the fork in his backpack and began making his way across the slope toward Xan.

"Whatcha' got?" he asked, when he reached her.

She held out her hand, showing a flattened six-inch piece of blue-gray rock, chipped to a sharp edge one side, dull on the other. It was obviously a stone tool, but not one that Shadow was familiar with.

"It's not an arrowhead. What is it? "

"I don't know. It's obviously some sort of artifact. " She handed it to him.

Shadow held the stone in his palm and ran his thumb across the face. It was surprisingly thin. He was amazed that the prehistoric toolmaker had been able to form such a delicate shape without breaking it in the process. He could almost sense the artisan trying to flake the stone to honor the spirit in it. Somehow, Shadow knew that the carver had failed, though he'd never tried to carve a stone tool in his life. It felt off-balance and, well, just not right. Surprisingly, he got no sense of age from it, like he normally did when handling Native American artifacts.

"I'm sure it's not a spearhead, maybe the blade for a tomahawk? "He shook his head. "If you don't mind I'll show this to Shawnee Jack. He'll know what to make of it. "

"Shawnee Jack? "

"One of the other rangers. He's really into artifacts and stuff, since this area is sacred to his tribe. "

"Why sacred? " She held out her hand and he gave back the stone.

Shadow gestured at the skies. "I guess it made the Shawnee feel like they were close to the gods when they came up here. They've got a cave in the park—we call it the 'Pow Wow Cave'—that they used for ceremonies and such."

"And this is a Shawnee artifact?"

"I'd guess so."

"And this Jack is a real Shawnee?"

"Yeah. Pure Shawnee, from what he's said. The tribe was re-located to Oklahoma way back when, but his family moved back here when he was a kid."

She looked at the stone, turning it over, then handed it to him again. "Okay, see what he thinks of it. But I'd like to keep it. I've got a few arrowheads I've found over the years, but nothing like this."

"It's a nice piece." He put it into his pack.

"What do you say we break for lunch?" she asked, looking up the slope toward a sheer escarpment. "I don't think we can climb much higher."

"Sure thing. I think I can arrange a table with a view."

When they had eaten—they had purchased sandwiches from a convenience store along the highway—Xan took a small pair of binoculars from a case on her belt and stood to scan the area in large, slow sweeps.

"Jeez, this is awful. It would take an army years to search just this part of the mountain."

Shadow remained sitting, making a dessert of a bag of M&M's. "Well, we had a small army here for a few days. Nothing like a lost child to bring out the Good Samaritan in folks. Never found hide nor hair, though."

She pulled the binoculars down a bit and raised an eyebrow. "What about that piece of Caitlin's bracelet you found?"

He shook his head. "That was right near where she was last seen and it didn't give any idea which direction to look for her. And there were a few signs that someone had been there. Nothing much, but. . ." He grimaced.

She dropped the binoculars to her side. "You didn't mention that before. What kind of signs?"

"There was a partial footprint and then I could see where someone had gone off trail."

"And you showed this to your superiors?" She peered at his face as though reading it.

"Hell, yes. But the signs were faint and the chief ranger wasn't convinced. He's made a couple of remarks and I think he's got me made out to be a glory hound. And I have to admit that there was nothing to actually connect your niece to any of it. Like I said before, I just had a feeling. An intuition. You know."

She sat down next to him. "I don't know. Why would your chief think you were out for glory?"

"Well, there was a problem at the last park where I worked." He crumpled up the bag and put the remaining candy in his pocket. "The state park commissioner ended up getting canned over it."

"And you caused it?"

"Not really. There were some murders at the park, and I figured out who did it. It was some guy found out that the commissioner was screwing everybody over and. . ." He sighed and held up his hands. "He sort of went nuts and started killing people."

She scooted over and put her hand on his arm. "Ew, you really are intriguing. Tell me all about it."

He looked down at her hand and then into her face. Her expression said that she would hang on every word.

Shadow had never been much for talking. But she nodded and smiled and said, "uh-huh," and, "yes, go on," and never let go of his arm. She soon had the whole story. Well, all he thought he could tell without her thinking he was crazy, anyway. And she did hang on his every word.

"How exciting." Her fingers squeezed. "And this all came about because of an aura you sensed around the first body?"

"Yeah." He nodded eagerly, having got himself all worked up with his own tale. "And that's why I said – when we first met - that my intuitions have a way of coming true."

"You're amazing, did you know that?"

Shadow could hardly believe his ears. No one had ever complimented him like this. But now what to say? "Thanks and I think you're the most gorgeous thing I've ever seen?" If only he could.

"Um, yeah, well, it all just sort of happened. I mean I didn't. . ."

"No, really. That's quite a story. It'd make a great book."

"Yeah, right."

"Seriously. Shadow, have you wondered why I could stay up here and search for Caitlin when my sister and her husband had to go back to work?"

"Um, not really." Maybe because I was too busy counting my lucky stars, he thought.

"I'm sort of self-employed."

"Uh-huh." I'm just glad you're here.

"I'm a writer." She looked him straight in the eye with a bemused smile. "I write true-crime novels."

Oh, crap, he thought.

CHAPTER TEN

"WAY UP HERE ON THE SIDE OF A MOUNTAIN?"

Luckily, from Shadow's viewpoint, Xan never mentioned writing about the False Cape experience he'd told her about. Her only focus was on finding Caitlin. But from some of the questions she asked during the days he joined her on her search, he figured it had to be in the back of her mind.

Most of the time, though, Xan explored on her own, since he had to work. She had a room at the Laurel Lodge, overlooking the canyon. April had turned to May and the days dragged on. He'd considered asking her out, but told himself it was too soon after her niece's disappearance. And he found himself wondering if that was the true reason. Although he had no problem with a woman having a mind of her own, he felt intimidated by this particular female. She came on awfully strong, now and then. He'd noticed her giving him appraising looks.

He'd showed the spearhead to Shawnee Jack, who'd been quite intrigued by it. "It's a flensing knife, made of hornstone."

"Flensing? "

"A butchering tool. It doesn't feel quite right to me, though."

"I wondered about that. It seems sort of off-balance."

Jack looked at him quizzically. "You know anything about flint knapping?"

Shadow shook his head. "Not me. Just a feeling."

"Oh." Jack turned the point in his hands. "Were there more of these lying around?"

"I don't know," Shadow said. "Xan found it. I never bothered looking around for more."

"Could you show me where she found it?"

"I guess. Why?"

"Well, um." Jack held the point close in front of his eyes, examining it. "If the knapper tossed it aside, unfinished, because he wasn't satisfied with it, you might have found a spot where he made his tools and weapons. There'll be more of them, maybe, nearby."

"But if they're all rejects. . .?"

"Still, I'd like to see where it came from. Will you take me there? Next time we're both off?"

"I guess, but. . ." Shadow couldn't understand Jack's seeming urgency. If there were more artifacts, they'd been there for centuries and would certainly keep.

"Good." Jack handed back the stone artifact. "Let's play some cribbage."

And then, on the last day of May, Shadow and Jack stood on the Kentucky side of the mountain. Xan had gone to New York for a couple of days, something to do with her publisher, so Shadow didn't mind making the trek with Jack. Still, he would have rather been with her. She'd finally admitted that the chances of finding her niece alive were slim to none, but she hoped for the closure of finding Caitlin's body. Shadow figured she'd give up soon. Another reason for not asking her out. Why get hung up on a woman who wouldn't be around long? He put his mind back in the present and led Jack to where the flensing knife had been found.

To his surprise, Jack said that they were a couple of hundred yards from the park, in Kentucky actually, and that it was a good thing.

"Why's that?" asked Shadow.

"Technically, all artifacts found in the park are to be turned in," Jack said. "I always do that, but I can keep anything I find around here."

He looked around and walked over to a jagged rock outcropping. "Hornstone." He examined the surface of the stone, about the size of a cow. "This is where he got it."

Shadow walked over and saw there was, indeed, a place where a slab of the stone had been chipped off. The surface where a section was missing showed much lighter in color. "It almost looks new," he said. "Like it's been done in the last year or so."

Jack gave him a quick glance. "I guess it does. A little." He dropped to his knees and touched the stone. "But, you know, you've got to consider how long would it take to weather."

"I haven't a clue," Shadow admitted. "It just seems recent to me."

Jack licked his lips. "Well, let's say the knapper broke it off a few hundred years ago. How old is the rock? Coupl'a million years, anyway. It would take quite a while for the scar to match the old stone."

"But. . ."

Jack stood abruptly. "Let's look around. We might be able to tell where the tool maker worked."

"Sure."

Shadow followed Jack back toward where Xan had found the artifact, wondering why Jack had seemed so nervous. He was probably right, anyway; nobody went around carving stone tools anymore. Still, Shadow remembered his initial impression the stone point had been carved not that long ago.

Jack suddenly stopped. "Here." He pointed at a low rock. "He used that as a platform when he carved."

"How do you know?"

"Look here." He pointed out various shards of rock, some small as cereal grains. He began picking them up. "He carved that point right here. Probably tossed it over his shoulder when he realized he'd screwed it up, then flaked another one. There's too many bits here to have come from that one artifact."

Shadow dropped to one knee and looked the site over. "But you said there might be a regular workshop here. Why would some guy stop and just carve one butcherknife?"

"Hmmm." Jack stirred the flakes of stone in his palm with the other hand, frowning. "And why throw the knife away because it was a bit off-balance? It would still work. Unless it was ceremonial."

"What do you mean?"

"Indians didn't only make arrowheads and tools to kill and skin game, Shadow." Jack tossed the shards down. "Sometimes they'd make a special artifact for use in some ritual."

"Ritual? Way up here on the side of a mountain?"

"What better place?" Jack waved a hand at the mountains. "My people lived all around here for hundreds of years and other tribes before them. Even if they were few and far between, compared to the modern population, they put their mark on this land over thousands of years."

"I just might join you more often," said Shadow. "I'd like to have a few artifacts. Just to hold them. Somehow they feel, well, soothing to me."

"That's what got me started on the whole cultural heritage thing. My brother found an arrowhead and then I wanted one and then it became a competition. We started looking into the history of flintknapping and tried some knapping ourselves. I'm not very good at it, though."

"Your brother?"

"He got pretty good at it. He said he could "feel" the rock."

Shadow knew what Jack's brother had felt. He felt it in wood.

"Where's your brother live?" he asked.

Jack grimaced. "He's dead. He got the prospecting bug and was always looking for gold or silver, or whatever. He was sure he'd strike it rich sooner or later." He shook his head. "He ended up disappearing in Alaska, looking for gold. His body was never found."

"Sorry to hear that."

"Shit happens," Jack said with a shrug. "Let's look around and see if we can find any caves around here."

"Why is that?" asked Shadow.

"There's probably more hornstone around here. And sometimes you find a cache of them in a cave nearby a source of good knapping stone, like a supply put away for some ceremonial purpose. But let's just keep moving along the slope and see what we can come up with." He turned and led the way.

Shadow followed, watching the ground in hopes of finding a spear or arrow point of his own. Jack had led off in the opposite direction from where Shadow and Xan had gone after finding the spearhead. The sun hung almost directly overhead, burning down on them. After a while, he became aware that he'd not likely find anything by following Shawnee Jack, who had the practiced eye of an experienced artifact hunter. "I'm going to move upslope, a bit," he said. "No use both of us covering the same ground."

"Suit yourself. Just give a holler if you find a cave."

Shadow was more interested in finding arrowheads or such than a cave. Half an hour later, though, something urged him to look at a particular outcropping—more of a jumble of huge boulders, really. Beneath them, he discovered a small cave mouth. It wasn't much, just a four-foot wide opening, sort of a right triangle and low enough that he'd have to stoop if he wanted in. Some time in the past, a huge rock had fallen upon a large rock sitting near a smaller rock and capped the space between. It wouldn't be very deep, most likely, and not nearly large enough for more than a few people to sit inside. Not worth bothering with. Except that he felt a hint of the same feeling he'd had before the weather had turned warm. And now he caught a whiff of a foul odor.

He looked around for Jack, but had lost track of him. Shrugging, he put his head inside the opening. It took a moment for his eyes to adjust as his nostrils filled with a lingering stench of putrefying flesh. When his vision adjusted, he saw a pile of bones, along with a small head with much of the flesh still intact, and the blonde hair still attached. Atop the skull was short blonde hair, lying face up. He took one look at the head and quickly averted his eyes to the rest of the small grotto. It looked to be jumbled red shorts and an off-white tee shirt, wrinkled, but lying flat. The design on the shirt was of two cartoon figures, waving. One was a humanized starfish and the other was something like a big-eyed bathroom sponge, wearing a tie and squared-off shorts. Above the sponge-character Shadow saw printing, some letters illegible due to the fabric being wrinkled: "WELC ME TO BIK NI BOT OM!"

Now he knew what a Sponge Bob was.

CHAPTER ELEVEN

"YOUR FULL NAME, PLEASE?"

Once Shadow had showed him the grisly scene, Jack called the police on his cell phone and then called Chief Ranger Martin, since the remains had to be those of Caitlin Bledsoe. After that, the Shawnee left to climb back down to the road, in order to lead the police up to the crime scene.

Shadow sat down outside the cave to wait. Without thinking, he shrugged out of his pack and rummaged for a pack of spice drops he remembered tossing in that morning. He found them and ripped open the bag.

Slowly, he sucked each piece of candy until it melted away. He stared off into the distance, without seeing. So, whoever had abducted the girl hadn't taken her to the highway. She'd been killed here, in the mountains.

In less than a year after becoming a ranger, he'd found four—now five— bodies and seen several more. And it seemed to be due to some resurgence of the mysticism he'd felt as a child, at least in part. Did coming back to his native Virginia have something to do with it? Had he been smothering something inside himself during all those years in the white man's world?

No matter the reason, he'd have to face up to it that he had changed, that his "intuition," for lack of a better word, had led him to yet another murder victim. In the first case, a murdered camper, he'd merely seen a body floating and felt evil when he'd touched the corpse. And he had trailed the footprints of a scavenging feral pig to the second discovery, but felt no "aura" until he'd actually approached the half-buried corpse. The third person had been killed on his own front porch. He'd felt the presence of the killer from nearby, just before finding the corpse. The last had been an FBI agent, shot dead in his car.

In the end, his sixth-sense had led him to identify the killer as someone with ties to Native American mysticism. But he'd gotten himself in a lot of trouble for his involvement.

And here he was again. Remembering how strong the presence had been at that spot alongside the trail where Caitlin Bledsoe had gone missing, he wondered if that spirit had drawn him to the cave. There must be some connection.

He stood and peered into the cave, hoping Caitlin's remains would speak to him in some way, but nothing came to him, other than the same sense of unease. He walked out a few steps and looked downslope. They couldn't be on the way up yet, he figured. Jack had probably only now made it to the road.

Returning to the cave, he got down on hands and knees and studied the cave floor, which was rock covered by a thin layer of dust. Tracks were there aplenty, chipmunk, skunk, 'possum – especially 'possum. Scavengers. If the killer had left any sign of being here, the varmints had obliterated it, as well as scattering the bones. It seemed to be an awfully small pile of bones, though.

Shadow wanted a better look but needed to get closer, but couldn't do that without entering the cavern and disturbing the crime scene, something he'd gotten in hot water for in the past. But he had to know.

He picked up a softball-sized rock in his hand. Reaching into the cave with it, he put it down on a bare area of rock and used it to support his upper body's weight without actually touching the ground. He raised himself up on a tripod formed by his boot-toes and right hand and, reaching out with The Claw, he stretched until his artificial fingertips came in contact with a rib bone.

The flash of otherness that he sensed did not surprise him. Much weaker than he'd expected, it whispered of foul and wicked actions as it tingled through The Claw into his wrist. Even though the sensation was far fainter than when he'd found the place where Caitlin had been ambushed, he felt a presence behind the aura. This girl had been murdered by an ancient demon of the north. Somehow, he could feel the identity behind that spirit more clearly now. Grandma Min's amulet, maybe?

Most of the larger ones of the legs and arms were missing, as though dragged off by animals. He recognized the butterfly shape of a hip bone and picked it up carefully with The Claw. Evil seemed to permeate his being. On the socket of the hip joint, he noticed several long scratches, as if some animal had dragged an extremely sharp canine tooth over the bone. But Shadow knew no animal had made these marks.

He felt a warm glow on his chest and realized it was Grandma Min's amulet. He told himself the warmth was just his imagination.

*

First to arrive, of course, were officers from Elkhorn City, the nearest town on the Kentucky side. Then came Chief Ranger Martin, Kentucky State Police patrolmen, local detectives, a state detective and a forensics specialist, pretty much in that order. Despite its remote location, the mountainside became cordoned off with yellow tape, isolating the cave and a hundred feet of the slope beneath it.

The two rangers filled in their boss, but Shadow wasn't willing to speculate aloud and their talk soon died down. Nothing much seemed to be happening. The first detective to reach the site had stopped any later arrivals from approaching the cave and cops of all types stood outside the crime-scene barrier. It took Shadow a while before he realized the investigation wouldn't begin until a detailed procedure had been established. No area would be entered until it had been thoroughly searched by experts. Shadow felt a small twinge of guilt, but he hadn't disturbed anything at all and felt sure no one would be able to discover he'd penetrated the cave first.

"Excuse me, Ranger," a voice came from behind him.

Shadow turned, swallowing the small remnant of a spice drop. "Yes?"

"I'm Detective Sergeant Bednarski, Jim Bednarski." He held out his hand.

The man, tall, thin, balding and with a beak nose, wore a suit. Shadow shook his hand, noting the detective's shiny shoes showed several deep scuffmarks from climbing the mountainside, and his trousers were dirty at the knees.

"Shadow Fletcher."

"How do you do?" Bednarski said, taking out a notebook. "You found the body?"

"Yes."

"How did you happen to come upon it?"

Shadow gestured toward Shawnee Jack. "He and I were looking for caves or artifacts. I just happened to notice that opening and looked inside."

"You're both park rangers, right?"

"Yes."

The detective began writing in his notebook. "Your full name, please?"

"I told you. Virginia Park Ranger Shadow Fletcher."

"Shadow, huh?" Bednarski smiled even more broadly. "I need your real first name, not a nickname."

"My name is H. A. Shadow Fletcher. I go by Shadow."

The sergeant smiled like a caricature of himself and squinched his eyes together, like they shared a secret. "Come on, I need your given name, for my report."

And that pissed Shadow off. "Fuck your report. I just told you that Shadow is my given name. A little girl's been murdered and you're all hot to trot about what the hell my name is."

Bednarski's false camaraderie turned to anger. "Listen, Ranger, I'm the investigating detective and I insist you give me your full name."

Shadow didn't reply. He simply locked eyes with the other man and stared, expressionless. Bednarski glared back.

It was Bednarski who broke. He glanced over at Martin. "I can get your name from your supervisor, you know."

Shadow turned and walked down the mountain.

John Bushore

CHAPTER TWELVE

"F.B.I.?"

"Shadder, the chief wants to see you over at HQ."

"Now? He usually doesn't want just one ranger in the visitor center."

Karen set down the phone. "He's sending someone over to replace you. Says some cops are coming up to interview you and he wants to talk to you first."

"Crap." Shadow threw down the report he'd been filling out and headed for the door. Once outside, he didn't bother with his truck, but walked across the road and down a sloping drive to the convention center and lodge, which included several buildings. Behind the restaurant, he walked by the restaurant's service entrance and the dumpsters. Wondering, not for the first time, why the park had been laid out so the ranger's had to smell the rotting garbage when nature surrounded them on all other sides, he went up the steps and opened the door.

"He's in there, waiting," said Doris, the secretary, waving him on with a scowl. A matronly, unfriendly woman, she then ignored him and went back to gazing into a computer monitor.

Martin's office door hung open. "Come in and have a seat, Fletcher," he yelled into the corridor. "And close the door behind you."

Shadow did as he was told, taking the chair directly in front of the chief ranger's desk. Martin was turned slightly away, drinking a something from a plastic cup. A torn, empty Alka-Seltzer wrapper lay at his elbow.

He emptied the glass and turned to face Shadow.

"Fletcher, do you have a problem with authority?"

"No, sir," Shadow answered.

"Then why is Detective Sergeant Bednarski coming up here to interview you? He says you refused to talk to him yesterday."

Shadow shrugged.

"You know," Martin said, putting his hand to his mouth and burping, "they warned me you might be a bit of a loose cannon. But your old boss stuck up for you, said it was probably just all the trouble they were having. You know what I

65

said?"

"No."

"I said we didn't have trouble up here. And we don't." Martin burped again. "But I made the mistake of telling this detective that you'd suspected abduction from the very start and now he's coming up here with an FBI agent."

Shadow raised his eyebrows. "This isn't federal land."

"The girl was taken from here and the remains were found in Kentucky. "

"Oh. "

"So, tell me," Martin said. "Why wouldn't you tell the man your name?"

"He pissed me off." Shadow squirmed in his chair. "Besides, I quit using my first name years ago. Shadow *is* my name, as far as I'm concerned."

Martin put the fingertips of both hands together and studied the arrangement. "So now we got trouble. And I'm a man who likes things all neat and orderly." He rearranged his fingers slightly so that he pointed at Shadow. "But I realize that whatever happened to that child is not your fault. And the best way to get things out of the way is to take care of business. You agree?"

Shadow nodded.

"So you cooperate with these guys. If they want to know your name, tell them your name. Give them anything you've got that might help. But don't be making things up or saying things you're not sure of, okay?"

"I wouldn't do that."

Martin considered Shadow closely. "I hope not. When they show up, use the room across the hall, and be sure to leave the door open. You can wait out front."

"Yes, sir." Shadow rose and walked out. Doris didn't bother to greet him again, so he checked his mail slot. Nothing. He sat down in one of the three plastic, uncomfortable chairs along the wall. Reaching in his pocket, he realized that he had left his bag of gumdrops over at the visitor center. He sat and fidgeted for a few minutes, then decided he had time to run back up and fetch them. He shoved open the door to leave and nearly bowled over Bednarski and a large, overweight black man with a shaved head and a gray goatee.

It was an awkward moment. Shadow knew he should apologize, but didn't want to start off on the defensive.

The black man made it easy. "Hey, you must be Fletcher. I never met anyone so eager to be interviewed." His deep voice boomed with friendliness. A wide, sincere smile lit up his face as he stepped inside and stuck out his hand. "I'm Agent Frank Langley, FBI." His voice was deep and mellow, with only a hint of a southern accent.

Shadow grinned and shook hands, noting the strength of the man. "Shadow Fletcher. But you already know that."

"Easy enough. Not too many blue-eyed Indians around." His voice was raspy, but his diction was precise.

"I guess not."

Langley, had a thick face that would fit in with the Rushmore Presidents, Shadow noted, as though he had been sculpted with a broad chisel. His mustache and goatee were flecked with gray.

"You know Detective Bednarski, I believe."

"I do." Shadow shook the hand of the detective, who glared at him.

"Is there someplace we can go?" he asked. "Or would you rather talk in the doorway?"

"This way." He led the pair along the corridor to the conference room across from the chief ranger's office. "Either of you want coffee or something?"

Both declined.

Shadow left the door open, as requested, so that his boss could hear the interview. Not that he cared; he had nothing to hide. The three men seated themselves at the end of the conference table.

"I'm glad they've got the FBI in on this," Shadow said to Langley, in the way of conversation.

"Why?" asked Bednarski. "Don't you think I can handle the case?"

Shadow turned to the detective. "I didn't mean that. Listen, I'm sorry about yesterday, okay. I'd just found a little girl's body and didn't want to play games."

"Sorry don't cut it," the detective growled. "I don't play 'games,' Ranger; let's get that straight. I don't care if your first name is mud, and *I'm* the man directing this case."

Shadow nodded with a wry smile. It was his own fault that Bednarski was miffed, so he'd just have to get over it and let the man do his job. Langley leaned back in his chair and smiled.

Bednarski took out his notebook and opened it in front of him. "Okay, I got your full name from your boss, so we'll skip that part so as not to get your shorts in a wad, Hubert. He also told me you claim to be some sort of tracker and think that the girl, Caitlin Bledsoe, may have been abducted."

"I don't claim to be anything," said Shadow. "But I can read sign and someone was up on that trail the day that little girl disappeared. So, yes, I think it's possible that someone might have taken her."

"Fletcher, that's a hiking trail in a well-used park, so of course there were other people up there. So what's your suspicion based on?"

Shadow told the two men about finding a partial print and following a faint trail to the creek.

"That's not much to go on," Bednarski said. "No blood, no signs of a struggle, anything like that?"

"No, but someone was waiting in ambush along that trail."

"How the hell do you get that from a couple of 'scuff marks,' as you called them?" The corner of the detective's mouth twitched, as though he were trying to control his expression.

Langley broke in. "Do you mind if I interject, Detective Bednarski?"

"Interject? Uh, sure, go right ahead."

Langley's face went professionally expressionless as he took out a notebook of his own. He opened it. "Ranger Fletcher, I've talked with Special Agent David Morrow, of our Norfolk office. I believe you're familiar with him?"

Langley turned to Bednarski. "Morrow was in charge of a multiple murder investigation. He interviewed Fletcher on at least two occasions and is convinced that the ranger is quite good in the wild, and did indeed discover the corpse of a victim by use of his tracking abilities."

So, there, thought Shadow.

The FBI Agent turned back to Shadow. "But he also said that you got in his way, always snooping around on your own. And you ended up finding the perp through pure-assed dumb luck."

Shadow had to grin at that one. "He's right about the dumb luck part. But I wasn't getting in his way. Just so happened that both my next-door neighbors got killed and a lady was murdered on my front porch. Kind of hard to stay out of the way, especially when I became next in line."

Shadow's grin vaporized as Bednarski said, "Well, I'd appreciate it if you didn't snoop around on my case. I prefer police procedures to dumb luck."

"Sometimes," Shadow said solemnly, as though instructing a child, "people let facts get in the way. A coon dog can use his smell to find a body, but someone has to put him on the scent and he has to take every flat-footed step of the trail. A vulture, though," Shadow gave him a smile as if they were playing poker and he was about to bluff with a pair of deuces, "can smell a stinking carcass from miles away and fly right to it." Damn, he thought, now why in the hell did I say that? And what in the world did it mean? He glanced over at Langley and was surprised to see him smiling raptly, as though amused by the tension in the room.

"Is that some kind of Indian shit?" Bednarski looked just as puzzled as Shadow felt. But he seemed even more angry than perplexed.

"Naw, that's just shit." Shadow leaned across the table and bared his teeth. "I wanted to see if you could take any more of it on or if you were full of it to the eyeballs already."

"Ranger Fletcher," Chief Ranger Martin said from the door, "I warned you."

Shadow sat back down. "Yes, sir." Damn military training. Would he ever be able to ignore a direct order?

Bednarski locked his eyes on Shadow and set his lips in a tight smile. "That's okay, Stanley," he said to Martin. "I believe Ranger Fletcher and I can agree to disagree."

Shit, thought Shadow, I should have known it. Everybody in these parts seemed to know everybody else. Martin and Bednarski were probably in the same bowling league or something.

"And I'm sure," Bednarski continued, "that Mister Hubert Avenging Shadow Fletcher knows enough to stay out of police business."

"And consider that an order from me, Fletcher," Martin said.

"I don't think," the FBI man broke in, "there'll be an extreme amount of police interest in this affair anyway. Certainly not my department. The only hint of abduction being a possibility is from Ranger Fletcher; everything else points to the little girl walking off the trail. Missing person gone bad. Little girl goes into cave for shelter, freezes to death."

But he seemed to be saying it "tongue in cheek."

"Really?" Shadow had learned that FBI agents weren't necessarily on his side; they tended to suspect everyone. Did Langley suspect the same thing he suspected? "If that's the case, why did you go to the trouble of asking agent Morrow about me?"

"You're the only one who's suspected foul play." Langley's smile never wavered. "And you're the one who found the girl's body. Besides," he shrugged, "we already have a file on you. I knew just who to call."

Shadow had to grin back; the FBI agent had exactly the opposite effect on him as the local cop. "And none of it good, I suppose."

"Au contraire, my good man." Langley waved away any unpleasantness. "You're a decorated veteran, disabled in the service of your country and Morrow said something good about you when all was said and done."

"Really?" Shadow raised his eyebrows in surprise.

"Yeah. He said you had an annoying habit of being right."

John Bushore

CHAPTER THIRTEEN

"THINK YOU COULD HANG AROUND A LITTLE WHILE?"

When will I ever learn? Shadow wondered as he walked back to the visitor center. It would be nice to have the authorities on his side for a change, but he had to go and shoot his mouth off. And he'd really like to find out sort of killer he was dealing with. He'd sensed evil before, but not like this.

He hadn't bothered asking about the cause of death, even before he'd pissed the detective off, because he knew they wouldn't know for sure, yet. There'd be an autopsy. It didn't matter. Shadow might never know exactly what had killed her, but he knew what had happened to her after death. Langley—and maybe Bednarski, too—would already know what the scratches on the bones meant and the autopsy would surely include it.

And he wondered if he'd ever see Xan again. He'd pretty much decided to ask her out for dinner when she returned from New York. But now she'd have no reason to return to The Breaks, in fact she'd have a reason to stay way. So much for that idea. Still, he felt glad that his finding of the body would give the closure Xan wanted.

So he was surprised, a week later, to find her on his doorstep again. "I just dropped by to thank you for your help," she said, waving away his invitation to enter the house.

"I'm sorry," Shadow said. "I just wish. . ."

Tears welled in her eyes. "At least you found her. Her mom and dad got to say goodbye."

Shadow's throat lumped up. He could think of nothing to say.

"She had a beautiful funeral." Xan pulled out an already damp and wrinkled paper napkin from somewhere and dabbed at the corners of her eyes. "All her classmates from school came." She looked away, to where distant mountains could be made out through the budding trees. "I just had to swing a couple of hours out of the way, on my way home, to tell you how much my sister and I appreciate it."

He nodded.

"Back to New York?"

She nodded in turn. "Yeah."

"Think you could hang around a little while? I'm off this evening and I'd like to take you to dinner."

She grimaced. "No can do. My editor is on my ass, I've delayed the manuscript too long already."

He heard himself sigh and wished he hadn't let that out. "Well, goodbye, then."

She raised an eyebrow and smiled thinly. "Whoa, Kemosabe." It's not like you'll never see me again. Just give me a raincheck. I'll be back this way now and then." Her smile became warm. "And you're someone I'd definitely like to see again."

Before he could respond, she stepped forward, put her arms beneath his and hugged him. His whole body tingled, primed for this moment by a few fantasies he'd had recently. Her lips met his and she kissed him. Just a short, polite peck, like a wife going off for the day. Still, it warmed him to the cockles, or somewhere like that.

"Mmm," she said, staring into his eyes. "You're just too hard to resist."

She kissed him again. This time she opened her mouth and went at it like she meant it. He put his arms around and held her close, returning her passion.

After a bit she pulled her face away and looked into his face. "Well, it wouldn't hurt to drive the rest of the way tomorrow, would it? After all, I'd be getting back to New York in the middle of the night anyway."

"So you'll let me take you to dinner?"

"I'm considering it." She brushed her lips over his. "Where would we go?"

His mind raced, but he hadn't eaten at any restaurants outside the park since being assigned here and didn't know of any fancy places, which a woman like this deserved.

"Uh, the Rhododendron, I guess." The restaurant serving the Lodge and Convention Center was a *nice* restaurant, but it was nothing special except for the panoramic scenery of The Breaks, just outside the window. And Nan had been staying at the lodge, eaten meals at the Rhododendron Restaurant many times. She was probably tired of the view.

"Sounds good to me," she said. "Can I use your bathroom to freshen up after the drive I've had?

"Sure," he said, and kissed her again, the feel of her lips like water to a man dying of thirst.

After a bit, she broke off. "Whoa, slow down, there, Hubert Avenging Shadow Fletcher. You'll have to feed me dinner so I can gain strength, if you plan to keep kissing me like that."

He could feel that he was grinning like a fool, but couldn't help it. "I plan to keep kissing you like that."

"Then let me get my stuff out of the car so I can get dressed for dinner," she said.

"Sure."

They broke away and Xan walked to her car. She got a small suitcase and a smaller bag from the car and returned. As Shadow opened and held the door for her, he saw Karen McCoy standing in her doorway, across the street and one house down. She'd obviously been watching for a while. Shadow shrugged and followed Xan in.

Shadow showed her where the only bathroom was and told her to put her stuff in the spare bedroom he'd prepared for Ashley. He wondered if he should offer to let her spend the night here, in the spare room, but decided it would be too bold. Maybe later, if things went smoothly.

He went and puttered in the kitchen, giving her the whole back of the house for privacy. He began putting dishes and clutter away, so she wouldn't think him a total pig. For a moment, he thought about having a beer, but decided he didn't want to wash the taste of Xan away. He heard the shower, then a hairdryer, which must have been hers, since he had never owned one.

After a bit, he heard the bathroom door open and Xan called, "Okay, I'm all done, if you'd like to get ready for our date."

He glanced up and caught a glimpse of long, shapely legs beneath a wraparound towel as she passed through the hall. No more than that, but it aroused him as he remembered how thoroughly she'd kissed him. And she thought of tonight as a *date*. There was little doubt their relationship was about to change.

He undressed in the bedroom, removing The Claw, but put his pants back on, without underwear, since he didn't have a robe. No need for one, long as he'd lived alone. Once in the bathroom, he removed his pants and slipped Grandma Min's amulet from his neck.

When he'd finished showering, shaving and brushing his teeth—hoping his breath had been fresh when Xan had kissed him. He pulled the pants back on, put on the amulet, then stepped out into the hall. The door to the spare room was still closed, so he called, "I'll be dressed in a couple of minutes, then we can go. You need anything?"

"As a matter of fact, there is something I'd like."

But the voice didn't come from the spare room. It came from the open doorway of his bedroom. He turned.

Xan sat on the edge of his bed, wearing only some very skimpy, sexy underwear. She got up and walked toward him.

She had put her hair back in a ponytail, which made her look five years younger and eliminated the efficient manner she normally maintained. It reminded Shadow of her twin, Cleo, who'd lost her daughter, and he felt a brief pang of guilt that they were about to do something that couldn't be further from mourning. He shoved it from his mind.

The long legs Shadow had glimpsed in the hallway were even sexier than he'd

73

thought. Above them rode lace panties that weren't much more than a thong, revealing as much as hiding. Then came a narrow waist, a pair of rounded, small breasts in a sheer bra, clearly showing her aroused nipples. Above that was the prettiest face he'd ever seen—except for Ashley's and that was different.

She opened her perfect lips and said, "In case you've forgotten, Shadow, the restaurant isn't open for dinner until an hour from now."

CHAPTER FOURTEEN

"CAN'T I JUST STAY WITH YOU?"

Round up the usual suspects, Shadow thought, looking around the courtroom. The same cast of characters again waited on the judge. And, this time, Shadow had left the jellybeans in his car.

Ashley, seated between her mother and the oriental lawyer, had turned and given her father a bright, cheerful smile when he'd passed them in the hallway on the way into court. And, surprisingly, Jessica had smiled too, though not so warmly. Did she have something up her sleeve?

The same female judge was present, sitting behind her desk, shuffling through papers. Everyone had waited in the hall while she took care of another case and then been ushered in to the courtroom. Now she looked up, caught the bailiff's eye and nodded.

"All rise," said the bailiff. When everyone had stood, he said, "Court is now in session, Honorable Judge Angela Thoroughgood presiding. You may be seated."

Judge Thoroughgood, looking somewhat out of sorts, Shadow thought, peered down at her papers as the court clerk read off the particulars in the case. When the clerk had finished, the judge addressed the court with a steely gaze. "As you all know, we are here to determine if there are changes to be made to the original custody agreement between the parties present." She turned to the clerk. "Do we have the report from Child Protective Services?"

"Right here, Your Honor." The clerk, seated near the judge, pointed.

Frowning, Judge Thoroughgood read through the report and when she raised her eyes to the court again, Jessica's lawyer raised his hand diffidently. The judge glanced at him and said, "Yes, Mr. . ." looked down at the papers before her, and then back to the lawyer, raising an eyebrow. ". . .Takenata?"

"I believe we can save the court a great deal of time, Your Honor."

"Oh?" The eyebrow arched higher.

"Mrs. Armistead," Takenata indicated his client, "has graciously agreed to the increased visitation rights requested by her former husband."

Shadow stiffened in surprise, noting that Ashley smiled over at him, nodding to say it was true.

". . .with one minor stipulation."

Judge Thoroughgood looked coldly at the Japanese lawyer for two seconds. "Come, sir," she said, "just tell us what the stipulation is. This is not court TV and you don't need to build tension."

Takenata visibly gulped. The judge was obviously having a bad day. She'd not been sharp at all in the earlier hearing. But it looked as though her temper wouldn't matter.

"Actually, it's more of a boon than a stipulation, Your Honor," Takenata said. "Mrs. Armistead wonders if her former husband would like to assume custody of the child for two weeks during the Christmas holidays, as he has not had the opportunity to spend any holidays with her for quite some time."

Yeah, thought Shadow. A year now since the divorce added to a year-and-damned-near-a-half deployed in Bumfuk, Afghanistan, well over the normal tour of duty. Christ on a crutch, Uncle Sam might have left him there forever if he hadn't got his hand whacked off.

And then he realized his young lawyer, Ellison, now standing, was speaking to him. "Well, Mr. Fletcher?"

Shadow rose and thought quickly, still a bit stunned by his good fortune. "Um, that's a long ways off, Christmas."

"Speak up man," the judge snapped. "I can't hear you."

"Er, I said that Christmas is quite a ways off, Your Honor."

The judge looked over at Takenata, who leaned over and murmured to Jessica. She tossed Shadow a quick, appraising glance as she whispered something into her lawyer's ear.

Takenata rose to his feet and nodded affably. "Mrs. Armistead would be glad to allow custody for a week before then. As well as full weekends, to the limit of one a month, as was mentioned in the plaintiff's request, I believe."

Ellison looked at Shadow, who smiled and nodded. The judge watched his reaction, looked back at Takenata, then turned her gaze to Ashley and smiled warmly.

"And how does all this sound to you, young lady."

"Oh, yes, ma'am." Ashley's face beamed as her head bobbed up and down.

The judge addressed the court. "Alright, the way I have it, Mr. Fletcher will have Ashley for two weeks during the holidays and one additional week in the meantime." She looked into the principals' faces. "And after that, twelve weekends and two weeks a year." She focused on Jessica. "One week at a time or all together?"

Shadow's ex-wife shrugged.

"To be determined by mutual consent of the parents." Judge Thoroughgood looked at the clerk. "Got that, Linda?" Linda nodded, writing.

"I so rule," said the judge, gathering her papers with a smile, and standing. "It's nice to see that *something* worked out well today, for a change."

"All rise," the bailiff intoned.

Except for the court officials, all rose and left the court. To Shadow's surprise, both his ex-wife and his daughter waited outside the courtroom. Ashley lunged forward and grabbed him around the waist.

Jessica's face showed not even a wisp of emotion. "Hello, Shadow."

"Hello, Jessica. I don't know how to thank you."

Her lips stretched into the illusion of a smile. "Don't. How do you want to work the weekends?"

Shadow thought fast. "Uh, I'll have to do some figuring and work out my schedule. It's over an eight hour drive, one way, so I'll have to do some planning and wangle some long weekends."

"Okay. Let me know." She began to turn away.

"Wait," said Shadow. "What about the week-long visit? I'll need to put in for vacation."

She looked back and shrugged.

"How about the last week in August?" he asked.

"Suits me." She turned her head back and walked away. "Come along, Ashley."

Ashley still hugging her father, said, "God, Mom, at least give me a few minutes."

"Five minutes," Jessica conceded. "I'll be in the car."

Ashley pulled away and looked up at him. "Oh, Dad, I'll be so glad to be with you for a while."

"I'm really looking forward to it, too. And I'll arrange for a weekend before August. I'll get a hotel room and we can go to Busch Gardens, or Colonial Williamsburg or King's Dominion."

"I've been to all those places a million times," Ashley said. "Can't I just stay with you? I've never been to the mountains, you know."

He smiled. "Whatever you like. I'm just glad your mother was nice enough not to fight it."

"Oh, that." Ashley squinched her face. "She's just using you. Wilford is taking her to Europe over the holidays and she doesn't want me dragging along like a rusty anchor."

John Bushore

CHAPTER FIFTEEN

"ANY COMMERCIAL SIGNS ON THE VAN, MAYBE?"

Shadow used The Claw to pick up a towel and wipe sweat from his face, his right hand gripping the bar of his new treadmill. He'd decided that it wouldn't do to be outpaced by all the other rangers, including McCoy, and bought the contraption at the same big-box store where he'd bought sheets and such for Ashley's bed. He put everything in the spare bedroom, figuring to move the treadmill out and have everything set for Ashley's visit.

The window-shaker air conditioner for this room was blowing out cold air, but it couldn't keep up with the late July heat, at two-thirty in the afternoon, even though trees shaded most of his roof. The rangers' quarters had no central air-conditioning, since cold was more likely to be the problem in the mountains. Still, it would have been fairly comfortable if he hadn't been trudging along at nearly four miles an hour with the treadmill on an upward slant. Whenever he got a chance, he hiked around the park, mostly sticking to the trails, but that wasn't enough exercise. He spent too much time behind the counter at the visitor's center.

He still had the feeling that someone—or something—lurked in and around the park. Nothing he could put his finger on, just a vague foreboding. But he'd been right too many times about such things to ignore his premonition of more trouble ahead.

He had placed a portable TV in the room because he knew that he'd give up on exercising if it became too boring. On evening shift that week, he had a choice of mid-afternoon soap operas or re-runs of old sit-coms or Judge Somebody-or-other who ran a pretend court. They had satellite TV service in the park, for the lodge, mostly, and he could have hooked up to that, but he'd not bothered. An old-fashioned antenna did just fine in the clear mountain air, especially at the park's altitude, since he'd made sure the TV had digital capability, even though he'd bought it used.

The phone rang. He thought about ignoring it. Probably McCoy, she'd begun calling him at home lately. She'd have some excuse about checking some paperwork or something, but she really only wanted to talk. Luckily, they were working different shifts this month and he'd been able to avoid her except for the calls.

Wondering if he should get one of those caller I.D. gadgets, he shut off the exercise machine and answered the phone, on the off chance it might be official park business.

"Fletcher," a voice came over the phone. "Brubaker here."

"Hey, Bru, what's up?"

"The Virginia State Police have called an Amber Alert. A girl was taken from a park in Elkhorn City, and a white van with out-of-state plates was seen in the vicinity."

Elkhorn City was the nearest city—more of a large town really—to The Breaks, just a few miles into Kentucky. "What do you want me to do?"

"The chief wants us to cruise the roads in the area, just in case. It's all according to the Amber Alert Plan to coordinate law enforcement agencies. Not a lot of cops in these here hills, we'll try to fill in the gaps."

"I'll be there in ten minutes."

"Don't bother," Brubaker said. "Just head out of the park, cruise around, and keep us updated on the radio."

"You got it." Shadow began to hang up and then said, "Wait."

"What is it?"

"You said 'out-of-state plates.' What state?"

"Dunno," Brubaker said. "But they were blue on white, so they weren't Kentucky."

"Gotcha. On my way." Shadow put down the handset and headed for his bedroom to strap on The Claw and throw on a uniform.

Minutes later, he was on the road in his truck, with the air conditioner blasting. He quickly called in to headquarters and let them know. At the end of the park's road, which meandered in a loop around the peak, he turned left onto 80 and started down the mountain. Highway 80 ran around the edges of the park, detouring around The Breaks in a horseshoe shaped bend. In this direction, he'd go around to the Kentucky side of the park, the area where he'd searched along the highway with Jack and Karen.

The road twisted and contorted like a snake with epilepsy, following the contour of the mountainside. Many tons of rock had been blasted away to build this two-lane highway, so he passed directly beneath many gray, jagged cliffs on one side and sheer drop-offs on the other. He hadn't spent a winter in these mountains yet, but could imagine these roads must become impassible at times.

There were no houses along this stretch, but dirt roads led away on both sides. He had no idea where most of them led. There was no doubt why they existed, though, for huge, coal trucks often came lumbering out of them for a slow, ponderous trip down the mountain.

Shadow soon found himself crawling along behind one of these behemoths, with no chance to pass. His only contribution to the Amber Alert was to watch the occasional vehicle going up in the opposite lane for a white van.

Steering the truck with The Claw, he picked up the radio microphone and thumbed the button. "Breaks 23 to Base."

Brubaker's voice came back."Go ahead, 23."

"About those blue-on-white plates. Any idea what states use that color, besides Virginia?"

"We looked it up. West Virginia and North Carolina are the only other nearby states who use that color."

"Any commercial signs on the van, maybe?" Shadow asked.

"Nope."

"Thanks. 23 out."

Shadow had mentioned ads because the mention of a white van, with out-of-state plates, had reminded him of "Boiler Ben" Bailey. He was sure Bailey's truck had nothing to do with the van today because it was bigger, a step-van, and the large lettering would have been hard to miss, but it jogged Shadow's memory. Maybe, soon as possible, he'd take a hike down the trail where the rangers had met Bailey and see what might be there.

His radio crackled into life with an all-units-bulletin. They had more information about the missing girl. Her name was Molly Johnson, she was nine years old and wearing only shorts, a bathing suit top, and flip-flops.

With a squeal and a hiss from its air brakes, the coal truck ahead pulled off on a section of gravel shoulder. Shadow got by, along with a half-dozen other cars that had been slowed down. He waved his appreciation to the truck driver for letting him by.

A mile later, he came upon another lumbering coal-hauler. Once again he slowed to a snail's pace. This was getting him nowhere; he couldn't see approaching traffic until it got by the truck. If a white van should go by, he wouldn't have time to catch the color of the plates—and, oh yeah, he remembered, North Carolina didn't have front plates, only rear tags. The only chance he'd have of seeing the plates would be in his rear view mirror, and even that would be unlikely on a sharp curve.

But then he came to the main highway and took another left. In minutes, he was in Kentucky. On this wider, somewhat straighter road, he would probably be able to watch plates. But then, traveling from Elkhorn City, the van had probably passed here long ago, if it had even come this way. Even so, coming around a sweeping turn, he saw a white-step van ahead, parked on the left. It was Boiler Bens' truck, but the lettering had been painted over with a slightly different shade of white paint.

Shadow went right on by. The van he was looking for probably wasn't a step-van. But still. . .

A few minutes later, Shadow had reached the outskirts of Elkhorn City. So, obviously, if the suspected van had been heading south, he'd missed it. Hell, it had probably been long gone even before he'd got the phone call from Bru.

So, what the hell? It was a long shot, longer than hell, but Bailey's truck had been parked along the highway the day after Caitlin Bledsoe had gone missing and there it was again, today. As soon as he found a commercial parking lot to turn around in, he spun back to the south.

He pulled onto the pull-off behind the step-van and got out of his truck. Taking a deep breath, he considered what he was getting into. For one thing, Martin had specifically warned him not to poke his nose into police business. But that didn't apply here, he was going to investigate inside the park and rangers were given police authority so that they could enforce the law within Virginia parks. But he'd been hired by the Commonwealth of Virginia, and he was now in Kentucky. He wondered if, working in an interstate park gave him police powers in this state. Should he call in?

Damn straight, he should. He'd learned his lesson the hard way. He reached back into his truck for the microphone. "Breaks 23 to base."

"Go ahead, 23." Shadow recognized Shawnee Jack's voice, and glanced at his watch. Just past four. Jack must have taken over for Bru.

"I'll be out of my truck for a bit," said Shadow. "No sign of a white van on the highway, but there's a suspicious looking vehicle on the side of the highway, and I'm going to check it out."

"If it's suspicious," Jack transmitted. "Maybe we ought to call in the police."

Damn, Shadow thought. It wasn't worth getting the police involved. He keyed the mike. "No, not like that, Jack. Remember that boiler guy's truck from a couple o' months back? It's here again. What's he doing on park land?"

"Oh. Ten-four. I'll let the boss know. Take a hand-held with you."

"Ten four," Shadow said. "23 out."

He clipped the portable radio to his belt and walked closer to the step-van. Ben—or whoever had painted it—had used several coats of paint, apparently, because the lettering and logo had been completely painted out. Shadow went over the guardrail. The bank on the other side was steep, as he'd remembered, but with enough irregularity to make his way down without sliding. When he reached the bottom, he set off down toward the river, taking the same trail that he, Jack, and Karen had taken when they'd encountered Boiler Ben Bailey for the first time. Because he'd been hitting the treadmill lately, and had become acclimated to the thin air, he traveled easily.

Shadow came to the river and it turned out to be one of those places where the river flowed across a shallow stretch, the marble-to-softball-to-basketball size rocks clearly visible beneath the clear water. The trail obviously ended here but, since he hadn't met Bailey, Shadow waded in. This part of the river was so wide that the current was only moderate, affording him an easy passage with the water never rising above his knees, giving a half-assed attempt to wash him downstream. On the other side, he found another obvious trail and forged on, climbing now, up a narrow and winding path.

He didn't know what he might find—didn't even know what he was looking for. There was not even a hint that big, slovenly Ben Bailey had anything to do with Caitlin's disappearance or this Amber Alert, but something was going on out here in the rocks. If nothing else, finding Bailey might ease the suspicion that had been. . .

Boiler Ben Bailey appeared without warning from behind a rock crag on the trail above. Each saw the other instantly, but Ben took two more steps while Shadow's unexpected presence sunk in. He had a large sack slung over his right shoulder. Turning to face the ranger, he let the sack fall with a muffled thud. Then he went for his gun.

Everything seemed to slow down for Shadow. If there'd been anything nearby to hide behind, he'd have dived for cover. His right hand reached for his automatic but he knew he'd be too late. He'd practiced shooting with his right hand again and again until he was almost as accurate as he'd once been with his now-missing left hand, but he'd never expected a quick-draw confrontation.

Dismayed, he knew that all Bailey had to do was clear the holster, pull back the hammer with his thumb, and then pull the trigger to fire his revolver. For Shadow, he'd have to draw his weapon and then, with two hands, pull back the slide to put a round in the firing chamber. Problem was, he didn't have two hands.

Even though he was a seasoned combat veteran, it took every bit of nerve he possessed to undo the holster strap, pull out his automatic and put it in The Claw. The Claw had no feeling whatsoever, of course, and it would be all too easy to drop it so he had to do it by sight. Every moment, he expected a slug to hit his body. As he began pulling the slide back, he heard Bailey's pistol discharge. At the same time, something hit the rocks a couple of paces in front of Shadow and then it whined off into the distance. Bailey had missed by a mile, not experienced enough to compensate for shooting downhill, it seemed. But he'd soon correct his aim.

Shadow pulled the slide all the way back and let it go. It slammed forward, chambering a round. As he transferred his weapon to his right hand, Bailey shot again and missed, the bullet buzzing over Shadow's head, this time.

Still feeling like he was stuck in a time warp, Shadow raised his arm, clicking the safety off. He leveled his gun as Bailey let go with another round. This one was wide of the mark, also, but Shadow couldn't tell where it went. He sighted carefully on his opponent's chest and pulled the trigger.

The passage of time altered again and everything happened at once. He heard his pistol fire, felt the recoil and saw the other man stiffen. Then he saw a flash from the barrel of Bailey's gun, only an instant later. And something smashed into Shadow's right side, just under his armpit, like a freight train.

The next thing he knew, he was lying on his back with a ball of pain in the back of his head, apparently where it had struck the rocky path. He had no feeling in his right torso or arm. If Bailey was about to finish him off, Shadow wouldn't be able to do a thing about it. It seemed easier just to lie there, but then the boiler man would win for sure, wouldn't he? And, from Bailey's violent reaction to the sight of an authority figure, Shadow suspected that the sack he'd been carrying might contain the little girl who'd just been abducted. Or, more likely, her body, since he'd seen no movement from the sack.

Rolling over on his left side, he pulled up his legs and managed to stagger to his feet. His eyes immediately went to Bailey, who lay still as death up the trail. Shadow's automatic pistol had been dropped when his arm went numb and he saw it, only a couple of feet away. Not knowing if Bailey might still be a threat, he considered picking it up with The Claw, but what was the use? He could hold the gun, no problem there, but he'd be unable to pull the trigger. Might as well grab it with barbecue tongs as The Claw.

Lurching up the trail to check on his opponent, he glanced down at his armpit. He couldn't see where the bullet had hit, only that his shirt on that side had a dark, spreading stain. His sleeve—he wore a long sleeve shirt, as he always did since losing his left hand—was also bloody and dark red droplets fell from his fingers.

Bailey's eyes looked sightlessly toward the heavens, glazed as they peered into the infinity of death. His hand still clutched the cowboy-type, single-action pistol he'd been so quick to use. Shadow stepped around him and looked at the sack. No outline of a small body showed. He nudged the sack with the toe of his boot. Packed tight, but soft, like it had been stuffed with grass or leaves. What the hell? Shadow could make no sense of the action taken by the man he'd just killed.

The main thing to worry about now, though, was bleeding to death. He walked over to a ledge in a nearby crag and sat down. Pulling the radio from his belt with The Claw, he considered how to manage pushing the transmit button down. It shouldn't be too hard to do. He'd gotten pretty good at using the prosthetic device, but it was hard to focus his attention on the task and his vision seemed a bit blurry. Then the lights went out.

CHAPTER SIXTEEN

"A LITTLE CONFUSED, ARE WE, MR. FLETCHER?"

Shadow awoke with a splitting headache. He could feel that his head and chest were both wrapped up tightly, and he was in a bed, elevated slightly at the head. A hospital bed, no doubt. He felt something around his neck, and realized it was the amulet Grandma Min had given him before he'd left for Afghanistan Not only could he feel it; he could smell it, a dry, dusty bitter odor. Where'd that come from? He'd tossed it out a long time ago.

Well, at least he'd lived through it. He hoped the Afghani kid had, too. He'd been a cute kid, not much more than four years old, with the black hair and brown eyes of Islam. Hopefully he was with his parents somewhere, with only bruises from Shadow jumping on him, putting his own body between the kid and the suicide bomber.

How could anyone do such a thing? Shadow didn't blame the terrorist for wanting to take out American soldiers—satanic demons, in the view of many Muslims—but couldn't he have picked a time when the kid hadn't been standing at the side of the road watching the Americans walk by?

It had all happened so fast. He and some of the men he commanded had been passing in front of the bombed out ruins of a shop when the man, dressed in loose-fitting, traditional Arab garb stepped out of the open doorway. There were only two things that separated him from any other Muslim on the street. The first was the look of fanatical glee in his eyes that he was about to kill his sworn enemy. The other thing was the fact that his hand was groping beneath his robe.

"Take him," Shadow had yelled and jumped to grab up the young Arab boy. He didn't bother to draw his sidearm. The young marines Shadow commanded, not much more than kids themselves, had faster reflexes than he did. There was a slim-to-none chance they could kill the terrorist before he set the charge off. If not, the boy would have a better chance of survival with Shadow's body armor between him and the blast.

At the thought of body armor, Shadow wondered why it hurt to breathe. The armor usually protected a man's vitals from an explosion and the helmet protected the head. Blast or shrapnel injuries were more likely to damage a man's limbs, if he survived. He flexed fingers and toes and everything seemed to be in working order—except for his left hand. No feeling at all.

"Ranger?" came a young, twangy, feminine voice. "Are you awake?"

A nurse, he guessed. So they must have shipped him to a hospital already. Was he in Kabul? Pakistan? Or had he been out for more than just a while and already in a U.S. hospital in Germany, maybe? But who was she talking to? Rangers were army, not marines.

He opened his eyes and found himself in a typical hospital room, although the furnishings and equipment, even the television up on the wall, looked worn and outdated. He turned his head first to the right, where he saw a filmy window providing a view of leafy trees, then to the left, where—behind the shapely figure of the blonde nurse, which was hard to look past—he saw a hospital bed, unoccupied. He smiled. At least he wasn't in intensive care; that counted for something. Been there, done that, and didn't want a repeat session. A repeat session? Why had that thought come to him? He'd never been in intensive care. Had he?

"How do you feel, Ranger?"

His eyes traveled to her face, where he saw concern in a pair of pretty blue eyes. But was she a nurse? A nurse, like a doctor, would be an officer and this woman had no insignia on her collar. She had a nametag on, over a very ample breast, identifying her as Maddy Parker, R.N. but it did not give her rank or unit. Nevertheless, she was a blond knockout.

"Why are you calling me 'Ranger?'" he asked.

"Well, you *are* a ranger aren't you?" She opened a clipboard that she was holding and looked at it. "I wasn't sure if, er, "Shadow" was a misprint or if it was really your name?"

"Shadow's my name. Lieutenant Shadow Fletcher."

Her eyes widened, left the chart and looked into his. "Okaaay," she said as though he were lying. "Can I call you Shadow?"

"Sure, I guess so."

"Do you remember what happened to you?" she asked.

"How the hell would I know? I just woke up." He knew he was being curt, but he didn't like being unsure of a situation. Never had, never would.

"Right." She smiled. "You got me there. Let's try another question." She held out a hand. "How many fingers am I holding up?"

"Three." And now he smiled. "I got hit in the head, huh?"

"Yep." She nodded and dropped her hand. "So how about telling me what country we're in."

"I'm not sure."

"Why not?"

"Well, the last thing I remember was the bomb going off and that was in Rutbah. But I figure I'm not still in Afghanistan because, if it's been awhile, I might have been air-lifted to Germany, and this sure as hell isn't sick bay on a carrier, so. . ." He stopped, surprised by the look of concern on her face. "Wrong answer, huh?"

"Sort of." She put down the chart and pulled something from a pocket. "Look, the doctor will be here any minute; I called when you first started to stir. Let me check your vitals. Hold this in your mouth." She put a thermometer in front of his lips.

He couldn't think of anything else to do, so he complied. Where the hell was he? The nurse had the same twang as Karen McCoy, and she. . . Now where had that thought come from? He didn't know anyone named McCoy, did he? Not Karen, anyway.

The thermometer beeped. The nurse looked at it, ejected the end of it, apparently into an unseen trash can by the bed, and then picked up his right wrist. Shadow raised his left hand up to wipe his brow, but it never got there. Because it wasn't there! His wrist on that side ended in a stump—fully healed for God's sake—with an odd nub of flesh near the end. Jesus H. Christ on a fucking crutch, where the hell was his hand?

The nurse took his blood pressure, but he was barely aware of the cuff inflating on his arm. His mind raced. Was he in the twilight zone or had he just plain, fucking, gone crazy? The bomb had damaged his brain! He'd had a perfectly good hand and now it was gone. Sure the bomb could have—must have—blown off his hand but how could it be healed in only. . .?

A white-coated man appeared in front of him, and he thought for a moment that they were about to take him away to the loony bin. But this wasn't an orderly. He was white-haired, distinguished looking despite a potato nose, and his name tag said, "P. Pflug, M.D." And again Shadow worried that he might be crazy because all he could thing of was, "Private First Class Pug-Fucking Ugly."

The nurse handed the doctor—Shadow noticed that he wore no rank insignia either—the chart she'd been holding when Shadow woke up. Dr. Pug-Fucking Ugly opened it, his eyes skimmed the contents, and then he closed it and handed it back to the nurse—what was her name? McCoy?

Then the doctor looked down, met Shadow's gaze and he smiled. "A little confused, are we, Mr. Fletcher?"

"Yes, we _are_ a bit confused, Doctor." Shadow cocked an eyebrow and gave the man a stare that stated he wasn't about to take any bullshit. "And I'm not a mister. I'm a Lieutenant. And I'd like to know what happened to my left _fucking_ hand!" Shadow noticed his voice rising to a high pitch at the end of his little tirade and realized he was on the edge. He wanted fucking answers and he wanted them fucking now.

The doctor looked down at Shadow's chopped-short wrist and then came back up. Now it was _he_ who appeared confused. "You, er, I have not the slightest idea about your hand. You were admitted to this hospital because you were shot in the chest and suffered damage to your skull, and you were wearing a prosthesis on your left arm. And you wouldn't let us take that whatever-it-is you're wearing around your neck. You have a concussion, sir; that is why you are a bit disoriented.

"A concussion!" Shadow laughed, long and hard, while the doctor and nurse stared at him. He couldn't stop laughing to explain he'd expected to die from the explosion. A gun shot wound and a blow to the head, however disorienting, was welcome news. He could sort out the contradictions between reality and delusion later on; at least he was ecstatically, wonderfully, fucking-goddamn alive.

Another man walked into the room and approached the bed as Shadow's laughter trailed off. The man, tall, thin, balding and with a beak nose, wore a suit. As he came on, he glanced down at Shadow with a scowl, then put his attention of Doctor Butt-Plug-Ugly or whoever he was.

The doctor shifted his gaze to the newcomer, back to Shadow's face and then he turned to face the man in the suit. At least it made sense that this man wore no rank markings; he was dressed in civvies.

"I heard he was awake," the man said in a nasal, annoying voice. "I need to ask him some questions."

Butt-fucking Ugly shook his head. "He's not up to that yet."

"Why not?"

The doctor began to answer, but Shadow broke in. "What do you need to ask me about?"

Maybe this annoying scarecrow knew more than the others. If he was investigating the suicide bombing, maybe he knew about the kid. "And who are you, by the way?"

"You know damn well, who I am, Fletcher. First you won't tell me your name and now you act like you don't know mine. It's Sergeant Bednarski, as you well know, and I'm getting sick and tired of your shenanigans."

Sergeant! If this guy was a sergeant, it didn't matter if he was a marine, army or even fucking air force. He'd show a little military courtesy, or Shadow would have his ass.

"That's *Lieutenant* Fletcher to you, Sergeant. And right now, I'm trying to decide whether to kick your ass before I put you on report. So you'd better damn well address me with respect and then get the hell out of my sight."

The man's eyes grew wide and he took a step back as if he feared that Shadow would actually leap out of his hospital bed. "You. . ." His face was turning red faster than a lobster cooked in a steam engine. "You. . ."

"I'm giving you an order." Shadow pointed at the door with the stump of his left arm. "Get the fuck out of here, Sergeant."

From the corner of his eye, he noticed the doctor and nurse looking at him in horror. He didn't let his gaze waver, though. He stared at the man with a look that would brook no insubordination.

The sergeant's mouth opened and closed like a carp sucking air from the surface. He didn't cave, as Shadow would expect any decent Marine to do, so he was probably air force. Undisciplined lot, that. The bozo-sergeant actually *glared* at

Shadow, a superior officer, before spinning around and stalking out of the room. Shadow considered calling him back and demanding that the bozo call him by his proper title, but he was tired. Very tired.

John Bushore

CHAPTER SEVENTEEN

"DID IT HAVE ANYTHING TO DO WITH THAT ARAB KID?"

Shadow awoke with a headache. He could feel that his head and chest had both been wrapped up tightly and he rested flat on his back in a bed. A hospital bed, no doubt. He felt something around his neck, and realized it was the amulet Grandma Min had given him when he'd visited her after the custody hearing. Not only could he feel it; he could smell it, a dry, dusty bitter odor. Just like the one she'd given him years ago, the one he'd ditched as soon as he got back on the base.

He wondered how he'd gotten here. He knew what had happened; that crazy boiler man had opened up on him for some reason. But he also knew without a doubt that he'd been unable to call for help before passing out. Why hadn't he bled to death in the rocks?

He opened his eyes. No one was in the room with him. A call button lay on the bedside table, but he ignored it.

Why the hell had it happened? Shadow had only wanted to see what Bailey might be up to. If the boiler man hadn't had anything to do with the abductions, why had he fired on sight? It was damn lucky that the big bastard couldn't shoot straight.

There had to be more to it, but Shadow hadn't a clue. It hadn't been a body in that sack and it sure as hell wasn't silver ore, or bars, or whatever.

The door opened and a nurse walked in, a pretty young brunette, a stethoscope around her neck. She looked at him and smiled in surprise. "You're awake."

He began to rise up his elbows and winced as a stab of pain lanced into his side. It didn't stop him, though and soon he was propped up. He looked up at the nurse, who seemed to be wobbling a bit.

The nurse rushed forward. "You shouldn't sit up. It'll make you dizzy.

"I'll say." He let her ease him back down. "How bad was I hit?"

"Not that bad, according to your chart." She pushed a button on the bed and it began raising his upper body. "The bullet went through the side of your chest, so it didn't hit any vital organs, but it broke a rib on the way."

He raised his left hand to wipe the sweat from his brow and came up short. The stump of his left forearm hung a few inches from his eyes. Damn, he must not be thinking as clear as he'd thought. How could he forget that he didn't have a hand on that side? When he'd moved, he'd felt a twinge of pain in his forearm and realized a needle was taped to his arm, with a tube leading to a bag of clear fluid.

"How long since I was shot?" he asked. The bed stopped moving, having raised him to a sitting position.

"A couple of days," The nurse, Linda James, L.P.N., according to her name tag, said as she walked to the foot of his bed and picked up a chart. She glanced at her watch and wrote something down. "They brought you in right after it happened. You were a bit out of it for a stretch. How are you feeling now?" She walked back over and placed the chart on a bedside table.

He again tried to remember anything about how he'd gotten from the place where he'd been shot, but had no memory to cover that period.

"How'd they find me?"

She pulled a thermometer from her pocket. "Now as for that, I haven't a clue." She stuck the probe into his mouth. When it beeped a moment later, she pulled it out, looked at it, then ejected its tip into a nearby trash can. She put it back in her pocket and picked up his right arm to check his pulse. After a few beats, she put his arm down and picked up a blood pressure cuff. "Funny, isn't it, how things go sometimes?" she said as she began putting it around his arm.

"Why funny?" he asked.

She smiled. "The whole hospital has been buzzing for two days and it's all over the news. They say you were searching for a missing girl, but it ended up with old Boiler Ben shot dead. . ." She paused to pump up the cuff. "And G-men swarming all over his marijuana crop." She began letting air out as she watched the gauge.

"Marijuana!"

"Of course, didn't you know? I thought everyone knew about Boiler Ben." She shook her head in puzzlement as she puffed up the armband. And then her face brightened. "Ah, but his farm was in the park. Nobody would tell you about it, not being a ranger. Anyway, no one in the hospital seems to have a clue about you. It wasn't in the paper and we couldn't ask you, for obvious reasons. You don't remember how you got here?"

"I have no idea."

"You didn't call for help?"

"I. . . I don't think so."

She paused and let the air out, while listening to the stethoscope. Then she said. "Well, you'll have to ask Dr. Pflug. He's on rounds, so I didn't bother to call him when I saw you were waking up. He should be here in a few minutes." She ripped the Velcro loose and removed the cuff from his arm.

"I'll ask him. But what's this about marijuana?"

"Old Ben's been farming it for years. He finds a holler somewhere out of sight and puts in a crop. He sells a little meth, too, and some other stuff, but he doesn't have a lab or anything. I doubt he works on any boilers anymore." She put up the blood pressure gear and picked up the folder.

Shadow wrinkled his brow. "And everybody knows about it?"

She opened the folder and took out a pen to write, but she paused and shrugged. "Everybody but the cops. And you park rangers, I guess." Now she smiled. "Nobody would narc on him to anybody who'd bust him."

"Why not?"

Again she shrugged. "People around here mind their own business. If someone wants to set up a still, or grow some weed or even build a meth lab, that's between them and the cops. Most of us won't take sides, less'n there's a relative involved." She began to write in the chart, dismissing him for the moment.

Shadow's mind whirled. Even if Bailey had been growing weed, why throw down on him? Because he'd been carrying that bag and was afraid Shadow would check it? Didn't seem worth killing a park ranger over.

The nurse snapped the folder shut. "I'll bring the doctor around in a few minutes. Do you need to use the bathroom or anything before I leave?"

"No, I'm fine."

"Okay, but don't try to get up unless someone is here to help you." She spun and walked from the room, dropping the chart back in its holder at the foot of the bed.

Shadow leaned back and relaxed. He was hungry as hell. How long had he been out of it? But the biggest mystery was: why was he alive? Why hadn't he bled to death out there in the rocks?

A man came into the room, obviously a doctor. He was a plain white-haired man, with a wide, overlarge nose, who looked tired. Nurse Ellison and another nurse followed him through the door.

"Good Morning, Lieutenant Fletcher," the doctor said as he strode across the room and pulled the chart that Ellison had written in.

"Lieutenant? Why would you call me that?" Was this someone he'd known while in the Marines?

The doctor halted beside him and looked down with a bemused expression. "You insisted we all call you Lieutenant." He chuckled. "I think that you believed you were a patient in a military hospital."

"Huh?"

"You apparently thought you were still in the army." He shook his head with a smile. "You did everything but make us salute."

"Marines," Shadow said absently, as he took in what he was hearing. He noted the man's name tag. Then he looked the doctor in the eye and shook his head. "I'm sorry, Doctor Pflug. I guess I was. . ."

The doctor dismissed his apology with another wave. "Don't worry. It's not like you were abusive—to the staff, anyway. Some folks are, you know, when they're a bit out of it."

"I didn't know. . ."

Doctor Pflug held up a hand to stop him. "First let's see how you're doing today." He formed a "V" with his first two fingers. "How many fingers am I holding up?"

"Two," said Shadow, wondering why the question seemed so familiar.

The doctor dropped the second finger, leaving only the index finger extended. "Now follow the tip of my finger with your eyes only. Don't move your head."

Shadow did as asked, and then submitted as the doctor gave him a quick once-over, asking questions as he did. As he moved various parts of Shadow's body around he asked, "How did you lose your hand?"

"I got caught in a bomb blast when I was in the Marines."

Pflug laughed. "That's not what you told Nurse Parker."

"It's not?" Shadow figured he'd probably embarrassed himself with some wise-ass remark and regretted it, even though he had no memory of a Nurse Parker.

"You said you'd lost it during astronaut training."

"Oh." That was the sort of thing he'd say when drinking.

"That bomb blast," said the doctor, "did that have something to do with the Arab kid? The one you kept asking us about?"

Geez, he'd really been a blabbermouth yesterday, by all accounts. "Yeah," he admitted. "I never found out if he survived the explosion." He had thought of the kid often, sort of hoping he hadn't lost his hand for nothing.

"Tough luck," Pflug said, but absentmindedly. "You seem fine today. Do you have someone to help you, change your dressings, that sort of thing?"

"I do," he said, although it wasn't true. Shadow didn't like being in the hospital, everyone fussing over him. He'd manage.

The doctor nodded. "I'm going to discharge you, then. I'll call Stan Martin. He said he'd send someone to get you.

Damn, thought Shadow. *Does every single person in these mountains know every other person?*

CHAPTER EIGHTEEN

"YOU? YOU FOUND ME?"

"Shadder?" came a voice from the door.

Shadow turned around. Damn it. "Hello, Karen. You come to get me?"

She walked into the room, followed by a gorgeous nurse, a blue-eyed blonde he hadn't seen before. Way too young for him, but still a looker. "Yeah," Karen twanged. "I asked Stanley if I could be the one to do it and he said okay. You got your stuff?"

"What stuff?" Someone had washed his clothes and the only sign of what he'd been through was a rip on the right side. He'd strapped The Claw to his wrist and put them on, with a bit of help from a nurse. "I didn't have a suitcase when I checked into his hotel."

Karen let out a hoot of laughter. "Shadder you're about the funniest feller I ever met. 'Didn't have a suitcase.' " She waggled her head from side to side. "Don't you beat all?"

"A laugh a minute." He twisted his face into a parody of a grin. "I'm ready to go."

"Let's get on with it, then," Karen said, as though anticipating something pleasurable.

The nurse stepped forward with the chair. "I'll have to wheel you down, Lieutenant Fletcher."

"Why?" He rose from the chair, noting the odd look Karen gave the nurse when she'd called him *Lieutenant* Fletcher. "I can walk." He placed a small bag, containing painkillers and antibiotics from the hospital pharmacy, in The Claw, where it would remain clamped.

"Hospital policy," The blond said. "We don't want you to fall down on the way out." She smiled. "The hospital is afraid of lawsuits."

Shadow noticed that her voice was nearly identical to McCoy's. So why did

95

she sound so much sweeter—so much more feminine?

"I've got my truck outside, Shadder," Karen said, stepping toward him and the nurse. "I'll help you into the chair."

"Sorry," the nurse said cheerily. "I'll help him. Policy, you know." She smiled at McCoy but she didn't seem friendly. Shadow had seen this sort of thing before, between females, and had never understood it. Why the antipathy? The two had just met, hadn't they?"

"Of course, Maddy." Karen's voice dripped syrup and Shadow realized that this probably wasn't a first meeting between the two women. He kept forgetting what an insular area this was.

The nurse parked the chair behind him and then came to his left side. She took his arm and The Claw and he wished there were nerves there. He'd welcome the touch of her fingers.

"Just sit down slowly," she said.

On the way down, he looked at her nametag. Maddy Parker, R.N.

Oh, shit, this was the nurse he'd told that he'd been lost his hand during *astronaut* training, of all things. He flushed, grateful for his dark complexion, knowing she must have him pinned as a bragging charlatan. But he'd never liked telling people how he'd *really* lost his hand. He put his remaining hand back to the chair's handrail, steadying himself on that side while she lowered him on the other. She seemed to be holding his arm quite close to her chest. Pleasantly close.

Once he had gotten in and put his feet on the footrests Nurse Parker—Maddy—put down, she went to the back of the chair. He expected to feel movement, but instead heard, "Oops, I forgot the brake." She leaned over his right side and her left breast pressed firmly into the side of his face as she reached down to release the wheels. The point of the name tag poked him a bit, but he didn't mind in the least. He inhaled the sweet, sexy aroma of woman.

"We need to get going," Karen said in a cheerful snarl. "Shadder's probably anxious to get out of here."

"Of course," Maddy said, straightening with an airy note of triumph. "Lay on, MacDuff."

McCoy glared openly, but turned and walked out of the room, Maddy pushing Shadow behind her.

And then they were off, with Shadow stifling his laughter. This backwoods, narrow-minded area of southern twang and moonshine likker was the last place he'd have expected to hear Shakespeare quoted. And Mccoy obviously had no idea that the phrase actually meant that Maddy was eager to do battle and would not yield an iota. Not only that, Maddy had said it correctly, not the usual misquote of, "Lead on MacDuff."

To his surprise, Maddy began humming, "Fly me to the Moon," as they walked down the hall. Was she letting him know that the astronaut remark hadn't fooled her a bit? Or was she hinting that she liked him? Or merely humming to irritate McCoy? He wished he could remember what they'd talked about besides his hand. She appeared to be a fascinating, complex woman. If only she weren't so damn young.

They reached McCoy's park-service truck at the side of the curb in what seemed an instant. Shadow was still grinning, thinking that it was lucky the small hospital only had one story. He had the humorous notion that, if they'd gotten on an elevator, these two women might have fought like caged lionesses. Surely it wasn't over him? He knew McCoy had ideas, but Maddy was probably only shamming to irritate the other.

The mid-afternoon air felt warm and inviting after the too-cold hospital room. Shadow welcomed the sun on his face.

McCoy opened the passenger door of her pickup truck and stood there waiting to help him in. But Maddy wasn't through yet.

She smiled sweetly. "I need to get him in the car. Policy, remember?"

McCoy's face hardened from granite to steel. She stood for a moment and then stiffly stepped aside.

Maddy had the grace not to rub it in. She put him into the truck professionally, not rubbing brazenly against him as she had done earlier. She'd already made her point to McCoy, Shadow realized, no need to repeat. But she squeezed his arm at the end and said in a low voice, "I enjoyed taking care of you, Lieutenant."

"The name's Shadow." He smiled. And thanks for taking care of me."

"My pleasure, Shadow." She flashed a smile that would have lighted up a stadium. "I washed your clothes for you. We wouldn't want an astronaut to look shabby, would we?"

Then she was gone and Karen stood looking after her with fury in her eyes, still holding the door open. When the nurse finally went inside, Karen came out of it, shut the door and walked around to get in. As they pulled away from the curb, she muttered, "I can't stand that girl."

Shadow cleared his throat. "I thought I, er, detected a hint of animosity there. You know her, I take it."

"She's a harlot." Karen's knuckles were white on the steering wheel.

He decided not to say anything. Hell, he didn't know what to say.

But Karen, driving the car as though it was a weapon, continued, speaking through clenched teeth. "She lives with another nurse; she and her parents didn't get along. I'll bet she hasn't seen the inside of a church since she moved out. And I know for a fact that she hangs around bars, drinking and dancing all hours. You can bet it doesn't end there." In a simpering voice, she added, "'I washed your clothes for you.' Slut!"

After that, they drove in silence. They left the small town within minutes and drove alongside the Russell Fork River, sometimes visible beneath them, at other times looping away from the highway. When they drove by the turn off where Boiler Ben Bailey had parked, Karen looked in that direction and seemed to soften.

"I forgot to ask," she said. "How you feelin?"

"Pretty good, considering. A bit tired, though."

"I'm glad you're okay." She glanced over at him, a strange look in her eyes. "I

97

just sat next to you and held a cloth to your side to slow the blood. I thought you'd bleed to death before help came and we got you back to the road."

"You? You found me?"

She nodded. "I saw the step-van, along with your truck, and I stopped to see what was up. There was no sign of you, though, so I was about to get back in the car. Then I heard the shots."

"Thank God you stopped."

"Yes," she said solemnly. "We need to get down on our knees and thank the Lord for succoring you in your time of need."

What in Hell was she talking about? God had suckered him? He wanted to ask but knew how sensitive she was when it came to religion. "Um, yeah. I guess."

"I had my whole congregation prayin' for you the last two days."

"Um, thank you," he said.

"Yes," said Karen. "I was the holy instrument what the Lord called upon to save your life."

Now it was Shadow's turn to go silent. He knew he needed to thank her for saving his life, but didn't know how to put it in words. He'd always avoided the subject of religion with her, and now she'd gone and woven herself into a miracle of the Lord. It dawned on him what the look she'd given him a moment ago had been. The pride of possession.

"Thank you, Karen," he said. "You saved my life." He took a deep breath. "You and the Lord."

When they got to his house, Karen insisted on helping Shadow in. She held his good arm as he went up the steps and led him to the chair in the living room. "Set for a while," she said. "You're probably done in from the drive, in your condition."

He was, but wouldn't admit it. "I'm all right."

"Would you like a cold drink or something?"

"That would be nice," he admitted. "There's some sweet tea in the fridge."

Karen disappeared into the kitchen and returned a minute later with two glasses of iced tea. She handed him one and then sat on the edge of the nearby sofa. "I'll just set a moment to make sure you're okay."

"Um, thanks."

"Anything I can do." She took a sip of her drink and smiled. She had that possessive look in her eyes again. "I noticed you don't have much in your refrigerator. Would you like me to bring you something for your supper tonight?"

He shook his head. "I'm going to bed and sleep until tomorrow. I didn't do well in that hospital bed. And they woke me up all the time." Why didn't she leave? His side ached and he was getting a headache

"Well, like I said, anything I can do. I'll check on you tomorrow morning."

He took a sip of tea and said. "There is something I'd like to ask you?"

"What?"

"Why do you suppose Bailey tried to kill me?"

She sighed, then shrugged. "He was probably higher than the space shuttle on meth, weed and who knows what else. Ain't no tellin' what he had in mind."

"Jesus," he said, then immediately looked over to see if he'd offended McCoy. He absorbed the information for a moment and then said, "One of the nurses said everyone knew about Bailey growing marijuana. Had you heard anything about it?"

"Not really." McCoy pursed her lips into a wry smile. I mean, yeah, I've heard rumors, but no one ever actually came right out and said that he was." She gave him a fleeting look.

"You never mentioned it when he said he was looking for lost treasure, though." He watched her closely now.

"Well, no."

"Why not?"

A hint of irritation crossed her features. "Why should I?"

"What happens in these mountains, stays in the mountains, and I'm an outsider, is that it?"

She squirmed in her seat. "Not really. You just didn't need to know."

"So you go to church and sing your hymns, but when somebody is peddling drugs that end up in the hands of kids, you ignore it." He saw her eyes mist over with tears.

"I'm sorry," he said. And he truly was; he shouldn't take his anger out on her. She'd saved his life for Christ's sake.

She sniffed. "I prayed for him." She took quick swipe at her nose with her knuckles. "And others like him." She finished her tea and stood up. "I'd better get going. I'm on duty, actually; Stanley sent me down to get you."

"Look, I shouldn't have said that."

She waved his words away, walking toward the kitchen with the empty glass. He heard ice cubes tinkle in the sink, a wash of water from the kitchen tap and then she reappeared.

"I'll check on you in the morning," she said, her lips set.

"Thank you," said Shadow.

She gave him a curt nod and left.

He sat for a few minutes, drinking his tea, then got up and went to the kitchen. Karen, he saw, had rinsed her glass and put it, upside down, in the drying rack. Surprised at her neatness in the shambles of his kitchen, he shrugged and immediately regretted it when his side twinged. He rinsed out his own glass, took two painkillers and then staggered into the bedroom, surprised at how tired he felt.

CHAPTER NINETEEN

"IS THAT THE KIND OF STUFF YOU EAT?"

He stayed in bed until morning, but the last couple of hours had proved restless. The same reason he'd lashed out at Karen had a lot to do with his nightmares. He'd killed a few terrorists, or insurgents, or freedom fighters, or whatever you wanted to call them, in his time, but he hadn't lost any sleep over them. At least not after the first one.

But Bailey was—had been—an American. One of the good guys. The "bad guys," the guys from the Middle East fought for a cause or a religion or whatever, at least they had a reason. But some of the "good guys" peddled dope around elementary schools. Other "good guys" were pedophiles. Others beat their wives. Most of them cheated on their taxes. But they were the good guys.

The bad dreams seemed to have come about because, now that he'd found out that Bailey was a drug peddler, Shadow felt a small sense of gladness about his death. He'd never felt that way about any of his foes on the battleground.

In the morning, he rose early as usual and, one-handed, put on a pot of coffee. There was a pile of newspapers on the kitchen table; Jack had probably brought them in. He went back to his bedroom and strapped The Claw on, since it was much easier to read the paper that way. He got a cup of coffee, then went through the papers as he sipped his coffee and chewed on a couple of stale cinnamon buns he'd pulled from the fridge. The oldest newspaper was from the morning after he'd killed Bailey. The Virginia Mountaineer, which covered the town of Grundy and the county of Buchanan, didn't hesitate to go over the state line for news items, so the abduction from nearby Elkhorn City, Kentucky was prominent on the first page. So was the killing of Bailey.

Elkhorn Man Shot to Death

Park Ranger wounded

He read that one first. Very few details, but they did have the identity of the dead man—Benjamin E. Bailey, age 43. And the article also said, "Authorities refused to confirm that Bailey was one of those sought, but still at large, after the bi-state drug raid last week, reported two days ago."

Shadow didn't remember seeing that article two days ago, so he went to the sofa and got that issue from a haphazard stack of old newspapers. He found the article and read it.

"Twenty-six men and women were arrested Friday and have been indicted of charges including drug possession and distribution, among others. In total, 78 charges were filed and unsealed by the court.

"Fifty-six individuals countywide were targeted in the effort and named in 172 sealed indictments.

"The task force asked that the names of those who escaped arrest last week not be identified until such time as those people are actually taken into custody and formally charged. The roundup of the other alleged drug dealers is still ongoing."

It sounded to Shadow like Ben Bailey knew they were after him. He'd painted out the distinctive signage on his truck and gone down to get one more bag of marijuana. Or maybe he'd made several trips before running into Shadow, clearing out the crop before changing his address to a more remote state.

So Bailey wasn't involved in the abductions. Shadow had never really suspected it, but at least he knew for sure now. And he had a motive for Bailey opening fire on him, too.

He went back to the newer papers, looking for details about the abduction. And he got them.

The girl, Megan Foster, 11, had been playing in a park, situated below the highway along the Russell Fork River. Shadow knew of the place, he passed it every time he drove to Elkhorn. It wasn't part of Breaks Park, being maintained by the county, but was nearby. She and her brothers and sisters had been playing hide-and-seek with some other children they met at the park. Megan had hidden and now the cops were seeking. Other than the speculation about a white van, nothing was known.

He realized that his coffee had gone cold with half a cup left. Getting up, he refilled it and nuked it. He hadn't eaten the second cinnamon bun, since the first one had been so tough. He picked it up, scraped the frosting off with his teeth and threw it in the trash. His side was sore from holding up the paper, so he went back into his room and got another pair of the pain-killers they'd given him and washed them down with water from the sink. By then the coffee was ready. He'd just set his hot-again cup of coffee down and was about to sit down when a knock came from the front door.

He looked through the living room and could see Karen McCoy on the porch. He'd half-expected not to see her; figuring she'd be mad at him for days. Him and his big mouth.

"Hold on a minute," he called, since the windows were open to catch the pleasant-smelling mountain breezes.

He went back into his room and pulled on pants, and a pair of slippers. He put on a civilian shirt, sort of, sticking his left arm through the sleeve and draping the other side of the shirt over his right shoulder. Even though his right arm had not been injured, he couldn't move it much without his side hurting like hell. He'd had a hard time getting undressed the night before, had actually ripped buttons to get his shirt off. And he seemed to have stiffened up in the night.

"Come on in," he called when he got into the living room.

"My hands are full," came the answer.

He went to the door and managed to turn the knob of the door with his right hand and swing it inward. Then he used The Claw to shove in the latch of the screen door and push it out and then stepped out to hold the door for her. She had a plate covered with foil wrap in one hand and a grocery bag – the paper kind with handles – in the other. She smiled and walked past him. Something smelled delicious.

"I figured you'd be up by now," she said, heading for the kitchen. "I brought you breakfast and a casserole for your supper. I'm working this evening, so you can just warm it up."

"You shouldn't have. . ."

"Oh, hush. I peeked into your refrigerator and there warn't hardly nothin' in there."

"You didn't look in the right places," he said. "There's cans of stew and spaghetti with meatballs and stuff like that in the cupboards. And the freezer is full of microwave dinners." He didn't bother to mention the drawer full of candy, which he considered one of the basic food groups.

She stopped pulling things from the bag and stared at him with reproach. "Is that the kind of stuff you eat?"

"Yep." He nodded emphatically. "Sticks to your ribs."

She snorted. "I'll bet." She nodded toward the foiled-over plate, which she had set down where he'd been sitting. "Here's breakfast, or lunch, however you want to look at it. Pancakes and sausage." She had a small container of syrup, half-used, beside the plate and a bottle of juice.

"It smells wonderful," he said.

"Tuna casserole for tonight." She pulled a covered dish from the grocery bag and headed across the kitchen. "I'll stick it in the fridge."

"Thank you." What else could he say? But he felt like his house had been invaded.

She returned to the table and folded the grocery bag neatly and slid it into the pile of newspapers, then straightened to face him. "I also want to tell you that you were right last night, about speakin' out when things aren't the way they're supposed to be. You're a good man, Shadder. And I would have told someone about Ben Bailey dealin' drugs, but all I knowed was rumors and gossip."

"I'm sure you would have," he said. "I was out of line. You're a good person and I know that. It's no excuse for saying something rude to you, but I've just killed a man and sometimes I get pissed off about the way things are."

"Then let's forget about it," she said.

103

He nodded. "Thank you."

"Now," she said, "is there anythin' else I can do before I'm on my merry way."

He swallowed. "Um, actually, there is, if you wouldn't mind."

"Whatever. I don't mind."

How far did "whatever" go with her? Shadow thought it might stretch quite a long way in his case. But he had little choice; he wanted to go out later and he couldn't go half-dressed. "Would you help me, um, put my shirt all the way on? I can't raise my right arm very high."

Her smile was so wide; he might have told her she'd won the lottery. "I'd be glad to, Shadder. That's what friends are for."

"If you can just help me get my right arm through the sleeve, I can handle the rest. I had to bust some buttons to get undressed last night."

Karen stepped quickly up to him. She looked him over. "Since you can't raise your right arm very high," she said, "we'll have to take it off and start over."

He realized she was right, and regretted asking.

She stepped around behind him and pulled the shirt off his right shoulder and unbuttoned the left cuff, which he'd been unable to manage. Sliding the sleeve down easily, she seemed surprised when she saw the straps that held The Claw on. "You know," she said, "you're so good with that thang that it's hard to remember it, 'specially because the hand part looks so dang real."

He smiled tightly. "They did a good job."

"I'll say." She ran her fingers over the harness, barely brushing the skin above it. It was a caress.

He stiffened. This was going to be more difficult than he'd imagined, if she kept that up.

But she didn't. She stepped behind him, all business now. He heard her shake the shirt out. He felt her arms brush against his bare side. Carefully, she eased the sleeve up his right arm. Then she held the other sleeve for him to put The Claw through. He couldn't see her, but he could sense her feminine presence so very close. And he could smell her, a clean, perfumed aroma.

She came around to his side and buttoned his right cuff. Then she stood in front of him.

"Hold out you left hand," she said.

I don't have a left hand, he thought. He said, "I can do that one myself."

She grabbed his wrist just above The Claw. "Now don't go all Mister Male-Independence on me. You axed me to put on your shirt and that's what I'm doin'."

Karen buttoned that cuff and then she was close, very close. Her hands touched him. She pulled his shirt together and this felt like another caress. Then she paused. Her eyes looked directly up into his. There was a questioning look on her face and a slight smile. Was she wondering if he would kiss her? He wasn't quite sure, himself. It would be all so easy at this moment.

He had admired Karen physically ever since he got to the park. And she was a nice person, a really nice person. But there was all that church stuff and she seemed so serious. But a kiss wasn't a commitment to marriage was it?

She lowered her head and began buttoning his shirt. He could smell the freshness of her hair. Her fingers were business-like but the motions were quite pleasant.

With a quaver in her voice, she said. "I never done this for anyone before. Not even my husband."

She could sense it. Same as him. As her hands went down, button-by-button it was so like the actions of a lover leisurely and erotically traveling toward *down there*. He noticed that her fingers trembled slightly. He felt himself beginning to swell *down there*.

Then the last button was done and she stepped back quickly. She let out a loud breath and, without looking at him, said, "There now. I think you better finish up for yourself."

He knew she meant tucking in the shirttail, of course. She looked at him then and gave a quick, embarrassed smile. Her face showed a flush.

He nodded, trying to keep his face expressionless. "Thank you."

"You're welcome." Her wavering smile dissipated. "Like I said, just let me know what I can do.

Once again their eyes met. Her hazel eyes were soft, and her lips were parted slightly. She was the prettiest thing he'd ever seen in a ranger uniform; that was for sure.

He broke the deadlock by looking over at the table. "I guess I should eat. That breakfast smells delicious."

"You're right." Karen looked at her watch. "And I better get to work." She returned her attention to Shadow. "Do you like meat loaf?"

"Sure," he said. If she was going to keep bringing food, he wouldn't mind. "Love it."

"Then you're coming to my place for supper tomorrow night."

Her place?

"I'm making meatloaf because it's my daughter's favorite," she continued. "And it wouldn't be Christian of me to let you stay home and eat out of a can."

"All right," he said. "I'll take you up on it." Karen didn't have romance on her mind, apparently, not with her daughter there. And she *had* saved his life.

Her smile beamed. "See you then."

"Right."

She left and he turned his attention to his breakfast, suddenly ravenous. It was still warm and quite tasty.

Afterward, he got in his Dodge and drove to the park where the latest abduction had occurred. The limited motion in his right arm didn't interfere with turning a steering wheel and the car was an automatic, so he had no problems. When he reached the park, he turned left, down a steep lane that came out in a parking area. The park, a wide flat area beside the river, had several small parking lots, connected by a gravel road. He stopped and surveyed the area. Behind him was the steep slope leading back up to the highway, across the river loomed a sheer cliff, a rocky crag soaring high above the churning river that cascaded from a narrow gorge on the left, tumbling over large rocks with a burbling roar. But the water soon slowed as it reached a wide expanse, almost a small lake of nearly still water. There was a sandy beach downstream—probably not natural—where a couple of kids had paddled out to an elephant-sized rock to play and dive. It was nearly noon and the sun blazed down hot, by mountain standards. At the other end of the narrow park, downstream, the Russell went into another gorge. The only way into or out of the park was the lane he'd just come down, unless you had fins, wings, or the feet of a mountain goat.

Shadow got out of the car and walked over to the rapids, stepping carefully across a field of rocks that he figured would be under water when the river ran high in the spring. Turning right, he soon came out of the rocks. From here on, it was solid ground, a park just like any other, picnic tables, barbecue grills, a small playground, and a restroom building. Shadow had expected to see crime-scene tape somewhere, but saw none. A police car was parked midway down the parking area, with a cop in it, though. Shadow briefly considered talking to the officer to find out what was known about the abduction. But, unless someone had seen the perpetrator, no regular cop could tell him what he wanted to find out.

He studied the ground as he walked, but merely from habit. There would be no sign left from the abduction, he knew. But if could find the place where it had happened, he'd know.

"Hi, there."

A woman walked a small dog in the other direction. A very attractive woman with a wide smile on her face.

"Hi," he replied, with a nod of his head.

"Nice day," she said.

"Mm-hmm." And then he was past.

Occasionally pulling jellybeans from his pocket—not that all easy to do, in his shape—and sucking on them, he reached the end of the park, at the downstream end, where the kids were swimming. An older woman, probably their grandmother, sat at a picnic table, watching them closely. She looked up as he approached, suspicion on her face. Shadow couldn't blame her for that. Everyone should watch their kids carefully and be wary of strangers.

He turned around and headed back for his car. There'd been no feeling of evil, or even unease, as he walked. He had no way of knowing exactly where the girl had been taken from, of course, but the park was so narrow that he must have gone by the spot. Since nothing had alarmed the sixth sense that warned him of malevolent spirits—only Native American ones, though, it seemed—he was inclined to believe this latest episode had nothing in common with Caitlin Bledsoe's abduction. As he drove back, he wondered why the hell women seemed so interested in him all of a sudden. Maybe it was only that he was single now, but that didn't seem enough to explain it. It felt wrong, somehow, in much the same way that the "Demon of the Mountain," as he now thought of it, seemed out of place in the park.

CHAPTER TWENTY

"IS THIS ANOTHER ONE OF YOUR HUNCHES?"

He'd not been home ten minutes when someone knocked on his door. Setting down his iced tea, he went to the door. He half-expected it would be Karen, come to mother him some more.

No such luck. Chief Ranger Martin had come to call. Shadow let his boss in and gave him a glass of tea.

"Do you mind if we sit down?" Shadow asked. "I've done a bit too much and I'm bushed."

"How are you doing?" asked Martin.

"Not too bad."

"You're lucky to be alive," Martin said. "There's plenty of men who've come across stills or meth labs in the hills and never turned up again."

Shadow nodded. "Damn lucky. If he'd been any kind of a shot. . ." He trailed off.

Martin took a sip of tea. "And it's no wonder you're tired."

Shadow raised an eyebrow. "Oh?"

The other man put his tea on a side table and leaned forward. "I'll get right to the point. I got a call a little while ago from Sergeant Bednarski. One of his men saw you walking around down at Riverside Park a while ago."

"It figures. I'm always getting on that guy's bad side."

Martin scowled. "Can you blame him? After the way you treated him when he came to see you at the hospital?"

Shadow wrinkled his brow and shook his head. "What in the world are you talking about? I haven't seen Bednarski since I talked to him and that FBI guy."

"What?" The chief ranger's eyes shot wide and bulged larger than usual. "He said you threatened him. You'd kick his ass, you said."

"Are you serious?" But Shadow was sure his boss was dead serious. "I swear

107

to you that I haven't had anything to do with Bednarski. And I *do not* go around threatening to kick people's asses; although in Bednarski's case I guess I just might make an exception."

Martin's ears were turning red and his Adam's apple bobbed beneath his receding chin for a moment while he tried to speak but nothing came out of him. Finally he said, "I—I've known Art Bednarski for all of my adult life and I can assure you, Ranger Fletcher, he is *not* a liar."

"I didn't say he was." Shadow was getting a little hot under the collar. "But I didn't threaten him, or even see him."

Red was now creeping up Martin's neck and coming down from his ears onto his cheeks. If he'd had a wig on, he'd have looked like a witch with that beak nose of his.

"And are you going to tell me that you weren't down snooping around that park?"

"I was there." Shadow could hear an edge coming into his voice and tried to control it. This guy was his boss. "But what of it? It's a public park and all I did was walk around."

"*Sergeant* Bednarski," Martin said, emphasizing the officer's rank, which somehow seemed to strike some sort of off-note chord in Shadow's mind, "Does not want you sticking your nose in police business. And neither do I, I might add."

"I'm sorry, chief." Shadow had played enough military politicking to know when to back off. "I don't want to cause trouble but I'm not messing with police business at all. I just wanted to see the place, get a feeling about what might have happened."

"A feeling? Is this another one of your hunches?"

Shadow shook his head, hating himself for backpedaling even though he knew his boss was right—basically. "No, sir, nothing like that – no hunches at all. I don't think this has anything to do with the Bledsoe abduction."

Martin's choler, which had begun to recede, darkened again. "We don't know she was abducted, she might have just crawled into that cave to stay warm and froze to death." He paused for a moment, as though recalling something. "And, if you're not the type to be getting into police business, why did you go after Ben Bailey? Drug-dealers are certainly police business."

Shadow breathed in, then sighed. Crap, they should be giving him a medal for removing Bailey. How many kids had the guy messed up over the years? But he minded his manners and said, "I wasn't after him, sir. I just noticed his truck parked in the same place as the day after Caitlin Bledsoe was. . . went missing and wondered why. We met in the rocks and he just started blasting away."

Martin pursed his lips, which gave him a weasel look. "So, you were checking to see if Bailey had anything to do with the. . . incidents. And isn't that messing with police business?"

Shadow sighed for the second time. "I just wondered what Bailey was doing, sir." He thought of something. "And he was growing pot in the park, isn't that *park* business?"

Martin's already puckered lips twitched around for a couple of seconds. "Yes, there is that. Look, Ranger, I try to be a fair man. Is there some way we can resolve this so you and Bednarski aren't at each other's throats?"

"I don't know, sir," Shadow answered, suddenly realizing he had subconsciously slipped into addressing his boss like a superior officer. And, in the military, your superiors didn't really care what your opinion was. Shadow figured that was the case here, too. He suddenly remembered the iced tea and took a sip, breaking eye contact with Martin. That usually worked to defuse a situation, he'd learned. He studied his glass.

There was silence for several seconds, then: "I'll tell you what, ranger. I want you to take a couple of weeks off. If you don't have the sick leave, I'll take care of it. Art said there was a doctor present at the hospital. I'll find out what the real story is and then we'll take it from there. Okay?"

"Yes, sir." He met Martin's eyes and smiled, shaking his head slightly. "I'm really not trying to make trouble for you."

"All right, we'll leave it at that, then." He stood and Shadow began to rise also. "No, you take it easy, mister. I can see how pale you are. I suggest you go to bed."

"Yes, sir."

The chief ranger went to the door, but turned before going out. "Fletcher, I do appreciate that you got that marijuana patch off my park. And I'm glad you won the shootout." He went out then, shaking his head.

Shadow held his breath until his boss was clear of the porch and then let out his laughter. Bednarski and Langley had obviously *not* told Martin what had happened to Caitlin Bledsoe after she'd died.

WENDIGO

CHAPTER TWENTY-ONE

"WHAT ARE YOU DOING HERE, ANYWAY?"

Shadow woke up in the early morning hours with a feeling of unease, slowly coming out of the deep torpor of his pain medications. He'd had a bad dream and. . . no, that wasn't it. There was a sensation of dread like he sometimes had when threatened in a dream and couldn't move to avoid it, but he hadn't been dreaming. Something was wrong, here in the waking world. He'd wakened this way in combat zones when he didn't feel sure about his position's safety.

Without stirring or opening his eyes, he took in everything around him. What had alerted him? Was it his supernatural sense or the instincts of a trained warrior? He took in all around him, the mattress against his back, the weight of his blankets, the air pressure on his skin, the faint glow of false dawn creeping into his room on the other side of his eyelids, and a faint, muffled sound of music. Music? The other ranger residences were far enough away that they'd have to really crank up the volume for him to be aware of it. Had he left the television on? Not likely.

At least it wasn't his "mystic" side that had awakened him. A strange sound would wake him in nearly any situation, as many dangerous places as he'd been in.

He opened his eyes and looked about. A light breeze came in the window that he'd left cracked open, stirring the curtains left by the house's previous occupant. The music came in the window, too. He slid out of bed and crept to the window. Without exposing himself more than necessary, he peeked out, but there was nothing to see.

It had probably been the music that had roused him, but he also felt a hint of something not quite right, but not in the in the same, supernatural sense that he often felt when confronted with evil. But there was nothing malicious about this. It felt good somehow, like a force of goodness that seeped into the world to counter the malignant spirits he'd sensed on occasion since leaving the service and returning to his native Virginia.

111

Nevertheless, the music was quite real. And inexplicable. He strapped on The Claw, and went to his closet, taking his pistol from the gunbelt hanging inside. He clumsily chambered a round, knowing he would be able to fire as needed, one-handed, after that first cartridge. In only his shorts, he moved stealthily to the door and let himself out, silently pushing the door shut behind him since he had no one to cover his back. It was dark in the hall but a glimmer of light showed ahead in the living room. He eased along until he could see that the living room was clear of danger, though there was less light here on the west side of the house than in his bedroom. He poked his head into the room and took a quick look to see if anyone might be on the porch and then pulled back quickly. The porch had been clear, but he'd seen a car parked out front—a car he'd never seen before.

Shadow stayed still, listening, with his back against the wall, for a moment. Nothing. He slipped down to his knees and edged his head out down low, where no one would expect and took a longer look. He couldn't be sure, but it looked like someone sat in the driver's seat. He pulled back into the hallway.

Now why in hell would someone be staking out his house? The only thing Shadow could think of was that Bednarski had sent some cop up to annoy him. Normally, Shadow would probably have crawled out into the room on hands and knees to reconnoiter from the windowsill for a clearer view, but his aching chest wasn't up to it. Time for a flanking maneuver.

Returning to his bedroom, he slipped on pants and shoes, then returned to the hallway. Whoever sat out front wouldn't be able to see in through the windows, not with the glow of the soon-to-rise sun coming from behind the house, so he slipped out along the living room wall and edged into the kitchen. Out the back door, noiselessly, and he was in his environment. In the house he'd felt penned, but now any combat would happen outdoors, in the cool morning air. He trotted straight away from the back of the house, out into the woods. Every step jarred his chest and a headache soon arose, but he ignored the discomfort.

Once into the trees, he turned. A wide circle took him around Jack's house, across the road, and then he was creeping up on the car from the rear, listening to the muffled oldies music from inside. He could tell the rear plate wasn't from either Virginia or Kentucky, but couldn't tell more with the sun in his eyes. Nor could he make out the occupant, other than the shape of a head. The goon in the car would have the advantage now, a glimpse in the rearview mirrors would reveal Shadow's advance if he left the bushes and crossed the road. But, from the partial view of the head and the angle, Shadow guessed that the person in there had put the seat back and was relaxing, if not asleep.

Shadow, remembering when he had dropped his guard and been captured by a killer months earlier, and how he had nearly been cut down by the seemingly innocuous Bailey, clicked the safety off his weapon. He eased out into the open and onto the road's dirt and gravel surface, his feet crunching slightly. He didn't worry about stealth, though; the music would cover his approach. The pistol held out in both hand and claw in a half-assed combat grip, he watched the head for movement. In what seemed to be no time at all, he stood next to the driver's window, aiming in at a familiar face.

At that moment, alerted by some slight sound, or a sixth-sense, Xan opened her eyes to see the muzzle of the gun pointed directly at her face. A scream erupted from her throat and she bolted upright, smashing her head on the car's roof. Shadow quickly dropped the gun to his right side, suddenly unsure just who he'd aimed a gun at. Was it Xan? Maybe it was her twin, Cleo. Whichever one, she lurched awkwardly forward in the reclined seat, desperately grabbing for the ignition keys as she glanced sideways to see if she'd have time to get away.

Shadow stood there, his mouth hanging open, as she started the car and reached for the transmission lever. But she abruptly stopped and stared out at him, eyes still wide with fear but slowly relaxing in recognition. The two stared through the glass at each other in amazement.

She shut off the engine, looked him up and down, and began to laugh. It was Xan, he knew then. Shadow had no idea if she was laughing at him, standing there like a doofus, or merely amused by the whole situation. He didn't see anything funny about it at all. Didn't she realize she might have been killed?

She opened the door and, still laughing, got out and rubbed the top of her head. "Jesus Christ, Shadow, what the hell are you doing?" She wore jeans, a sleeveless shirt, and sneakers.

"Umm. . ."

Xan pointed at him. "You should see yourself. Half naked, bandaged up head and body like the long-suffering hero in a bad movie, standing in the road with a gun in your hand."

"What are you doing sitting out here in the dark?" he asked sternly.

She stopped laughing and took a breath. "I got to the park just," she glanced at her watch, "a half-hour ago. I figured you'd be getting up right at dawn, like you always do, so I decided to take a nap rather than disturb you. But I didn't know," she gestured at the gun, "that you weren't accepting visitors."

"Christ, I'm sorry." He stepped closer, reflexively putting his arms up to hold her, but the weight of the gun in his hand stopped him. "I didn't mean. . ."

"No," she said. "Don't apologize." She swallowed, still trying to compose herself. "That was *so* stupid of me. I write about crime, but I never thought I'd be looking into a gun barrel myself."

"Why were you laughing?"

Looking at him, wide-eyed, she shook her head. "I haven't the slightest idea."

But Shadow knew. He'd seen a lot of young men react in many ways to their first brush with death set, every nerve on edge with the fight or flight rush of adrenaline. When the tension went away, the body had to relax. Some laughed. Some cried. Some even fainted.

"What are you doing here, anyway?" he asked.

Now Xan looked insecure, maybe even embarrassed. "I learned you'd been shot, but I didn't know how seriously. I—I came to see you." She put out her hand and touched the dressing on his chest. Now she looked concerned. "Were you hurt bad?"

Shadow found himself wanting to tell her that, yes, it was bad; please keep looking at me like that and don't stop touching me, either. "Only a scratch, really," he said. "I fell and hit my head, though, and I was woozy for a while."

"And here I've got you standing out here with no shirt on. Damn, that was a stupid idea not to just check into the lodge and just come surprise you, instead. Let's get you back inside." She reached back into the car for her purse, then shut the door. Taking his right arm, ignoring the pistol, she urged him toward his house. "Who the hell did you think I was, anyway, that you came out ready to shoot?"

"I–I'm not sure." And he wasn't. What had he been thinking? Was he getting paranoid? Just because one man had shot at him didn't mean he was a target for everyone that came near him. "But you never answered my earlier question. Why are you here?"

"I told you; I read that you'd been shot." She helped him up onto the porch, as though she considered him an invalid, even though he'd just been running around in the woods.

"And. . .?"

"And what?"

"And why," he said, as she opened the outer door and reached for the door knob "would that concern you enough to drive way up here in the boondocks?"

She twisted the knob. "It's locked."

"I came out the back."

She turned and they stood inches away from each other, faces close. Her hand still gripped his right arm, soft and warm.

"Why are you here?" he asked again, hoping for the right answer.

Xan's lips parted. She breathed deeply and looked him in the eyes. "I missed you, Shadow," she said.

Their faces came slowly together and their mouths met. Her lips were tender and sweet. She put her arms around him and once again he became aware of the weight of the gun in his hand. Her mouth opened as the kiss intensified and he stiffened a bit as she squeezed him. She pulled back.

"Oh, I'm sorry," she said. I didn't mean to hurt you."

"You didn't. Look, let's get inside. I enjoy kissing you, but I'd rather do it without a gun in my hand." He grinned. "Sort of ruins the moment."

She smiled. "To tell the truth, I'd forgotten all about the gun."

"Come on." He took her arm this time, and led her around back, into the kitchen.

"Let me put this cannon away," he said. "I'll be right back."

Once in the bedroom, he put his pistol away and then took a deep breath. On the way back to the kitchen, he stepped inside the bathroom and quickly brushed his teeth, looking at himself in the mirror.

Xan stood by the counter. "I put water in your coffee-maker," she said. "But I don't know where you keep the coffee."

"Right here." He went to a cabinet.

"Okay, I'll be right back. I need to use the bathroom.

WENDIGO

Shadow made the coffee and then rinsed some mugs and spoons, remembering Xan's only other time in his house. The kitchen didn't look any neater than it had before, he had to admit.

He'd cleared the table and put out cream and sugar by the time she returned, and stood by the coffee-maker, waiting.

"Coffee will be ready in just a sec'," he said.

"Sounds good." She put her purse atop a stack of old newspapers on a spare chair. "There was a new toothbrush in that closet, so I used it. Hope you don't mind."

"Not at all." Hell, no, he didn't mind.

Xan walked by him and sat at the table. "I'm sorry that I hurt you when I hugged you." She raised an eyebrow. "Only a scratch, huh?"

"Yeah. The bullet just grazed me. Problem is that it cracked a rib on the way past."

"What exactly happened?" she asked. "How in the world did you get in a gunfight with a drug dealer?"

Shadow told her the story, but limited it to the actual confrontation with Bailey. He left out the part about the Amber alert; it might upset her so soon after her niece had died. When he'd finished, he realized the coffee had been ready for a couple of minutes so he poured them both a cup and sat down opposite Xan.

"And you don't think this Bailey guy had anything to do with that little girl who's missing?"

He looked at her in sudden interest. "How'd you know about that?" So much for keeping it from her.

"I heard about the Elkhorn City abduction—it hit the national wires, you know—so I logged on to the on-line edition of local newspaper and there you were. They said your injuries were 'serious,' but didn't go beyond that." She watched Shadow put two spoonfuls of sugar into his cup. "Don't you have any low-cal sweetener?"

"No," he said. "Never touch the stuff. And I don't think this girl's abduction has the slightest connection to your niece."

"What makes you say that?" She pursed her lips in obvious distaste as she added a tiny amount of sugar to her coffee.

"I went to the park where this latest thing happened. I didn't feel a thing out of the usual."

She stirred her coffee. "You still think there was something weird about Caitlin's dea. . . disappearance?"

"I do," he said, after sipping from his mug. "I still feel like there's something evil hanging over this park and Caitlin won't be the end of it."

She sipped her coffee and made a face. "Ugh. What do you put in this stuff?"

"Sorry," he said. "I should have remembered to tell you that I add a bit of salt to my coffee grounds." *And I probably forgot because she's the first person to share morning coffee with me in a long, long time*, he thought.

"Salt? Who in their right mind puts salt in their coffee?"

115

"It's a military thing," said Shadow. "It helps replace the sweat you lose when you're stationed in a hot climate. I got used to it and it doesn't taste right without salt to me anymore."

She grimaced at her mug and then looked up at him, brightening. "Tell you what. I'll buy breakfast at the lodge. Unless you've got them putting salt in their coffee, too."

"You've got a deal." He stood up, delighted with the idea of breakfast with Xan. "I'll throw a shirt on." He reached for her coffee with The Claw, planning to dump both mugs into the sink, but missed and knocked it over. Xan got up quickly and managed to avoid being scalded, but it was a near thing.

"Christ, I'm sorry," he said. "Did I get any on you?"

"No." She grabbed a napkin and tried to stop any more from running off the table. "Don't worry about it."

He grabbed a dishtowel off the counter and began wiping the spill up, but she took the towel from him. "I'll get this; you get dressed."

"Okay, if you insist." He walked to his room and removed his shoes, put on socks and then put the shoes back on. As he squirmed and contorted to get a shirt on—long-sleeved, of course.

Her kiss was still fresh in his mind. Why had she missed him? Sure, she'd said she'd be back, but to actually *miss* him? What was that about? Still, he'd often thought of her.

He got the shirt on and managed to button the front and his left sleeve, but there was no way The Claw could handle buttoning the other cuff. What the heck? At least he'd managed to get into the shirt.

When he returned to the sink, Xan had cleaned up and washed the mugs, not to mention the other dishes that had been awaiting cleaning.

"All set?" she asked.

"Let's go." He began picking up his keys, wallet and other stuff with his hand, putting everything into his pockets.

Xan obviously noticed his flapping cuff, for she stepped close and said, "Here, let me button that for you."

His senses heightened by her nearness, he obediently held up his arm. Her hand shook as she did the fastening. When she took her attention away from his sleeve and looked into his face, he took her into his arms.

"I missed you, too."

This time there was no gun hanging from his hand to distract him. He enjoyed the sweet, yet intense feel of her lips and the kiss became passionate. She slid her hand under his shirt and rubbed the skin on his back. He tried to do the same, but his right arm wouldn't lift high enough and caressing her with The Claw would be about as exciting as scratching her back with a rake. Her hands roamed over his torso, arousing the nerves of his flesh wherever she touched. He felt helpless and frustrated, his hands unable to do the simple things that a man should have done to her while locked in a kiss such as this.

She began undoing his shirt buttons and pulled back, breaking off the kiss.

WENDIGO

There was a pouncing panther in her blue eyes. He reached out and tried to lift her shirt, but failed. Xan stepped back and, for an instant, he thought she was breaking things off. But she smiled and said, "Here. I'll do it for you."

She pulled the sleeveless shirt over her head and tossed it onto the nearby sofa. Her black bra was a lacy affair, low cut to show plenty of her orange-sized breasts. Shaking her head to straighten mussed hair, she grinned sinfully. Her hand went to her bra's clasp, between her breasts. "And I don't think you'd be able to undo this, either." She twisted and pulled the cups from her breasts.

Shadow would have moved forward to caress them with his good hand, but now he didn't even have one hand to explore her body with. So he dropped down, leaned forward and kissed her nipples, one after the other.

"Ooh, look Ma, no hands," she exclaimed. She reached up and cupped both of her breasts, offering them to his eager lips. The nipples quickly engorged and her breathing became rapid.

"Stop for a moment." She straightened and pulled the bra completely off and tossed it to join her shirt. She began carefully removing his shirt, taking time to caress him here and there as she did. "Let's get you out of this."

As soon as the shirt cleared his arm, it went flying. She came up against him, nipples brushing his lower chest, and offered her lips again. He complied. Her arms went around his waist and hugged him gently. He put his left arm around her shoulders and drew her closer.

He reached his right hand between them and tried to unbutton the snap on her jeans. The waist was tight and it resisted. He might as well hang a "handicapped" sign around his neck. But Xan's brought her hands from behind his back. She assisted him in undoing the snap, then pulled down her zipper. And now Shadow found out that he couldn't get his hands inside there.

Xan broke off the kiss, breathing hard. "There is no graceful way to get out of these tight jeans, standing up. Take me to your bed."

"Um, it's sorta messed up."

"Like I care?" She looked down, undid his belt buckle and unsnapped his pants. "I'd take you right here on the floor." She pulled down his zipper. "But you're not up to that." She dropped her hand and squeezed him through the fabric.

John Bushore

CHAPTER TWENTY-TWO

"WHY DID YOU DO THAT, GRANDMOTHER?"

Shadow wished he could put his fingers in his ears to block out the noise from the radio, but he was driving. How could anyone stand listening to this awful racket? But he could tolerate it, he told himself; at least he was with Ashley. Not that she'd talked much since he'd picked her up – Jessica hadn't been there to see her daughter off, of course – and he wondered if Ashley was sorry to have agreed to spend the time with him now that she was in his old Dodge. She probably felt like she was slumming it, especially because she couldn't plug her I-pod or whatever into the Dodge's radio like she apparently could in her mother's car.

Shadow had never seen Armistead's house before. It had turned out to be less than the mansion he'd expected, but not by much. It was a huge, old brick Federal-style building with maybe an acre of land, behind a high brick wall fronting the street in a fashionable neighborhood. He wondered how long it would be before Jessica convinced Armistead to move into something more expensive and ostentatious—and cheesy unless Jessica had changed her tastes.

The only time that Ashley had shown any enthusiasm was when he had told her that they'd be staying overnight with Grandma Min before traveling back across the state to The Breaks. Shadow wasn't about to drive two eight-hour stretches in one day. Besides, he had something to ask Grandma Min.

Despite the music, he couldn't help grinning, thinking of all that had happened during the last week, which had been spent with Xan. After they'd ended up in bed together the morning she'd shown up, she hadn't bothered to check into the lodge. She'd stayed with him. He'd never met a woman as independent and strong-willed as her. And she certainly was a wonderful lover, unabashed yet considerate, taking him to thrilling heights he'd never reached before.

She'd decided to go back to her home in New York when she learned that Ashley would be staying with him for the next week. Shadow had agreed that it

119

would be for the best; he didn't want to jeopardize his new custody privileges if Jessica should learn that Xan was living with him, if only temporarily.

The tension with Chief Ranger Martin had eased up considerably. He'd talked with Doctor Pflug and learned how the latest confrontation with Sergeant Bednarski had occurred. He said he had actually chastised Bednarski for trying to interview Shadow in the hospital so soon after being shot. Shadow had asked Martin to ask Bednarski if, now that a second girl had been abducted, Shadow might get a copy of the Bledsoe autopsy report, but it was probably a wasted effort.

But another sort of trouble had come up. In the excitement of his new relationship with Xan, he'd forgotten about agreeing to dinner with Karen McCoy and now she was royally pissed. He couldn't blame her, either. Never before had Shadow had so much trouble with women.

He'd decided not to tell Ashley that he'd been shot; he could see nothing to be gained by doing so. That was a closed book, as far as he was concerned. His wounds had mostly healed, Bailey was dead, and he no longer felt any sort of menace around the park. Which was a relief, since his daughter would be staying there with him.

When they pulled into Grandma Min's yard, she was waiting on the porch rocker. Shadow guessed that, if he were alone, she'd have feigned disinterest like she had on his last visit. But Grandma Min loved her only great-grandchild too much for that. She stood and waited as Ashley bolted out of the passenger door and ran up to hug her beloved Grandma Min. Shadow smiled, pulled their luggage out of the back seat and carried it past the two chattering females, into the house.

As he set the bags down in the bedroom hallway, he heard Grandma Min shout. "Hubert! Light off the barbecue, we're having a feast tonight."

He grinned. A "feast" meant that Grandma Min would cook freshly caught herring over hot coals, along with ears of corn cooked inside the husk, and buttered corn bread. She considered using the barbecue as cooking in the "old way."

That night, while Ashley watched TV in the living room, Shadow and Grandma Min sat at the kitchen table and talked.

"You're sure it's gone?" Grandma Min asked.

Shadow shrugged. "I haven't had a hint of it, whatever it was, in weeks."

"Hmmm." Grandma Min took a sip of beer and swished it around in her mouth, considering. She swallowed and said, "Maybe it went back north."

"Maybe." He took a pull on his own can. "But there's something else that I've been feeling."

She ignored his statement. "Well, it's a good thing it went away. I wouldn't want you to be taking my great-granddaughter to that place if it was anywhere's about."

"Don't worry," said Shadow. "I'd never let anything happen to her."

"Hmmph."

Her sound wasn't derisive, she just meant that it was a given that a father would protect his daughter.

Shadow pressed on. "But there's something else I've been picking up on. Subtle, hard to define, but friendly, and I wouldn't give it a second thought, except for some odd goings-on."

"Not important then," she said. "Just so the other thing's gone."

"Did you put something else in that amulet you made for me?"

"Now why would I do something like that?" She stood abruptly. "I need another beer."

And now Shadow grew sure he was on to something. If she wanted a beer, Grandma Min would always have Shadow fetch it for her. She was avoiding the subject.

She came back and popped the can's top. "That herring sure makes you thirsty." Putting the can to her lips, she put her head back and gulped several times. From the living room, Shadow heard, "Okay, that's the final performance for tonight. And that means it's time for you to e-mail or text-mail in *your* vote to decide who gets to come back next week."

He finished his own beer, then went to the refrigerator. Over his shoulder, he said, "You know, I never knew I was so damn appealing to women."

"Don't say damn, Hubert," Grandma Min said quickly. "Of course women like you. You're a good looking boy."

He returned to the table, set the beer in front of him and wrapped both hands around the cold metal, without opening the can. Fixing his gaze on his grandmother, he said, "I met a good-looking smart woman back when that little girl went missing. She couldn't get enough of me, right from the start."

Grandma Min stared right back at him. "Smart girl, knows what she wants."

"And there's this lady ranger who's got her sights set on dragging me to the altar."

Min dropped her gaze and fiddled with her can of beer. "Nothing wrong with that."

"And then there was this young, sweet nurse that took care of me in the hospital."

Her eyes came back to meet his. "Hospital? Why were you in the hospital? I warned you. . ."

He raised one hand to quiet her. "I'll get to that later. It had nothing to do with, well, what we were worried about." He looked at her quizzically. "But this nurse—and she was a real looker—came on to me like a bitch in heat. And, despite what you say, I'm far from irresistible."

"Yes, you. . ."

He shushed her again. "You put some sort of charm into that amulet, didn't you? Something that has nothing to do with the thing from the north."

"It was for your own good," she snapped. "It's not right for a man to be living alone, way up in the God-forsaken mountains."

"How would you know?" Shadow allowed himself a smile as he opened his beer. "You've never been there." He knew what her answer would be—same as it always was.

"I've never been to hell, neither, but I know I don't want to go there."

Yep, right on target. "Why did you do that, Grandmother?"

She turned and looked out the window as though she could see something besides darkness. She sighed. "How else can I expect another great-grandchild?"

He didn't have the heart to scold her. Possibly because his heart was sinking so quickly. Xan was the best thing that had happened to him in a long, long time and it had only occurred because of an old witch's magic. Would she still be attracted to him without that magic?

Sliding the thong over his head, he pulled off the charm his grandmother had given to him and slid it over. "Take it out," he said. "Whatever love hex you put in there, take it out."

CHAPTER TWENTY-THREE

"WHY WOULD SOMEONE WALK THROUGH SNOW BAREFOOTED?"

Shadow glanced out his bedroom window, saw an unexpected, light covering of snow on the ground and wondered why summer had taken its sweet-ass time leaving. Days had dragged after he'd taken Ashley back to Richmond. After an exciting, sex-filled week with Xan and a satisfying visit with Ashley, he couldn't help being sorry that he didn't have a home. The dwelling he lived in was nothing but a house, with wood, shingles, and even most of the furniture owned by the state of Virginia. He began his morning routine of getting ready for work, idly thinking.

Ashley had enjoyed staying in the park. She'd never seen the mountains before and delighted in walking the many trails with her dad. They'd ridden the park's horses, pedal-boated in the small, man-made lake, explored the beaver pond, and fished for trout in the Russell Fork River with newly-purchased fishing gear. It made Shadow uneasy to let her out of his sight, but she spent some of her time with a boy her age, whose family's motor home filled a site in the nearby campground. She'd gone swimming with the boy in the park's pool—after Shadow had quickly purchased a swimsuit for her—a couple of times and even spent an evening at the family's campfire with Shadow's reluctant approval. It was not that she was with a boy that worried Shadow, the opposite sex became attractive to every young person, sooner or later. No, he just felt a general nervousness about not being close enough to protect her, if that malevolent aura settled over the park again. But he was just being an old woman, he'd told himself. And, sure enough, nothing had gone wrong, Ashley and the boy had swapped phone numbers and Shadow had driven her back to Richmond, while she texted back and forth with the boy.

As Shadow, in full uniform, sat at the kitchen table with a cup of coffee and a couple of glazed donuts, he reflected that Christmas remained several weeks off, despite the gradually dropping temperatures. But then Ashley would be back for a couple of weeks and he could show her the beauty of the mountains in their white winter coats.

Xan had called with the wonderful news that her latest book had been sold by her agent, but also with the disappointing revelation that the publishing house's editor wanted major changes and she'd be busy getting it done. She promised Shadow that they'd get back together, though, as soon as she could break free. But, now that Shadow knew why he'd attracted her in the first place, it sounded as though she were putting him off, as kindly as possible. Shadow wondered if he'd been too hasty, telling Grandma Min to get rid of the love hex.

The love charm's effects had worn off Karen McCoy, no doubt about that; she wanted nothing to do with him now. She was barely civil on those occasions where they worked in close proximity. The only congenial person around was Shawnee Jack and he seemed pre-occupied. Even when he did feel like playing cards, his former gusto was gone. Why, he barely even tried to cheat anymore. Shadow had indirectly asked Jack what was wrong, but he only mumbled something about his brother and an old Indian legend.

Shadow sort of half-considered attempting to look up that nurse from the hospital, but he knew he was just being silly. That girl was too young for him. He hardly knew her. What would she see in him now that the love charm was gone? And even though Xan had put him off, probably for good, Shadow knew he would feel like he was cheating on her.

So Mr. Hubert Avenging Shadow Fletcher might as well resign himself for a long, boring stretch until he could see Ashley again. He put his coffee cup in the sink, opened the drawer and stashed candy in various pockets, then went out the door.

That's when it hit him. The feeling of other-worldly danger was back, almost imperceptible but unmistakable: the thing from the north. It must be in the air; he'd not felt it indoors with the windows closed. Shit! Had something happened overnight?

He locked the house—a task he'd been not bothering with lately—and headed for park HQ with snow still falling, feeling there must be *something* wrong. Sure enough, when he got there, there were ranger trucks in all the spots in front of the office and more vehicles out in the lodge's parking area. Every ranger in the park must be here, even the temporary help that would be let go when the park closed after Halloween. He parked as close as possible and walked briskly to the office.

When he opened the door, he was surprised to see that only Doris occupied the room.

"Where is everybody?" he asked. "What's up?"

Doris glanced disapprovingly at Shadow, then at her watch. "Breakfast, if you can manage to eat in ten minutes. The class will start at eight, but there's probably still plenty of food at the buffet."

Oh, crap, how could he have forgotten the first-aid class? But that was supposed to be Wednesday, wasn't it? He must have gotten his days mixed up somehow. He backed out and headed up concrete steps toward one of the restaurant's back entrances, retracing his work schedule in his mind. Everything had been so boring lately that every day seemed no different that the last.

When he entered one of the restaurant's dining rooms, several nearby rangers nodded amicably. A table at the rear held a portable serving line with yellow flames dancing from cans of Sterno beneath pans of food. Baskets held rolls, bagels, breakfast buns and other goodies. A great urn of coffee towered over all else.

He decided not to bother with the food. Normally, eating two breakfasts would have suited him fine, but not today. A quick look around the room showed that he was probably the last to arrive. He'd have to sit in one of the chairs at the front tables, sparsely occupied because of the danger of being chosen to participate in some first-aid demonstration or other. But then he saw Jack, gesturing him over to an empty chair by his side.

Shadow gave him a "just a minute" sign and got himself a cup of coffee, then went and sat next to Jack.

"What's up?" he asked.

"Good luck. You seen today's paper?" Jack gestured at a folded newspaper sitting in the middle of the table.

"No, not yet," Shadow answered.

Jack pulled the paper to him, opened it up, then folded it so the top of the front page was up. It was the State Journal from Frankfort, the capital of Kentucky. Jack put his finger next to a column headline that read <u>Child Killer Arrested</u>.

Shadow snatched up the paper and began reading. The police investigation of the abduction of Molly Johnson had led to a known pedophile and sex-offender in West Virginia. The man had confessed, and police were hopeful that he'd soon lead them to the body. Nothing was mentioned about the Bledsoe case.

"This is probably the end of it." Jack said. "I'll bet this asshole killed both girls."

Shadow could feel his lips tightening into a thin line. "I doubt it."

"Why?" Jack seemed to be intently studying Shadow's face.

"This guy was a sex-offender," Shadow said, "and the Bledsoe girl wasn't taken for sex."

Jack seemed quite concerned. "How could you know that? There wasn't nothin' but bones left. Did you get a look at the autopsy report?"

Shadow shook his head. "I don't need an autopsy report. I don't think this pervert has anything to do with our—I mean Sergeant Bednarski's—case."

"What makes you think that?"

"Nothing really." Shadow shrugged. "Just a hunch, I guess. But how you been doing? You figure out that thing about your brother and an old Indian legend?"

Shawnee Jack tensed, looked Jack in the eye, then sighed. "No, not yet. In fact, I think I must be going crazy. You see, I found some tracks that. . ."

A loud voice came from the front of the room. "Alright, gentlemen, it's time to get started. I'd like to introduce. . ."

An hour later, the CPR students were waiting their turns, grouped around a pair of rangers who were putting liplocks on Resusci Annie and compressing her chest, when Chief Ranger Martin broke in.

"Ladies and gentlemen, we're going to have to postpone this training session. We have a missing child and I want all of you all out at campground B to search for him. Ranger Williams, here, will give you the details."

Shadow was familiar with Williams. He'd been here long enough to know all the rangers, though not all the park staff.

"We're looking for..." Williams consulted a paper in his hand. "...eight-year-old Mark Kaminski, wearing a blue snowsuit and black rubber boots. He was playing out with a bunch of other boys from the campground, participating in a snowball fight. When the fight ended, Mark never came back to his parents' RV. They searched for nearly half an hour, assuming he'd gone into another RV with one of his friends, but couldn't find him. They called us at..." He looked at his watch. "...Nine-oh-two."

"Okay, men, get moving." said Martin. "I want you to pair up and drive to Campground B. We'll fan out from there."

Shadow and Shawnee Jack teamed up, of course, driving to the campground together in Shadow's truck. The snowfall had stopped and the day was warming up, melt-water beginning to drip from the trees, since flat snowflakes melt quicker. Once at the campground, Shadow could see that many people were wandering, helping to search. When all the rangers had arrived, about twenty of them, they milled around for a few minutes, as Martin stood and talked to the worried-looking parents.

Finally, Martin addressed his men.

"Okay, men. I want you to fan out through the campground. He's probably nearby. Keep in sight of the man you're paired with. Luckily, there'll be tracks with all this snow around. When you find them, call me on the radio and we'll re-assess the situation. Get to it."

"Excuse me, Chief," said Shadow. "Where was the snowball fight going on?"

Martin looked to the parents.

"Over there," the father said, pointing to the northeast. "They were having a snowball war with the other campground's kids."

Shadow turned to Jack. "Let's go." He turned and walked in the direction the father had indicated, getting a head start on the others, who were discussing who would go where.

"You thinkin' what I'm thinkin'?" Jack asked.

Shadow nodded. "Yeah. If he's in the campground, someone would have found him by now, with all the fuss that's been going on. So he went north. It's not rugged, so even a little guy could get quite a distance away, maybe running for a place to hide and getting lost. . ."

Jack interrupted. "Lost? He could follow his tracks back."

"You never had kids, right, Jack?"

"Nope."

"Kids don't think for themselves," Shadow explained as they walked. "They rely on their parents. He could panic and be running around in circles or just be sitting on his butt somewhere, bawlin' his eyes out. If so, he'll be found pretty quick. But I want to make sure there's nothing more to this."

Jack looked at him sharply. "Why would there be more to it? This is a little boy, not a girl."

Shadow snorted. Jack knew better than that. "Split here," he said. Go maybe a half-mile and then circle back toward me. If there's tracks, we follow. If not, we've cut the search area down to almost nothing."

Jack nodded, not bothering to point out that they'd just been ordered to stay within sight of each other. "Sounds like a plan."

Jack went east by northeast. He would have to go through the northern part of Campground C. Shadow went north by northeast, and was soon clear of Campground B. As agreed, he went a half mile, then turned to hook up with Jack. Almost immediately, he found the footprints.

They weren't the prints of a child in boots, but the marks left by extremely large, bare, human feet. There was no doubt about it. The outlines of the toes were clear, all except for the two smallest toes on the left foot. They seemed to be missing. Deep down in his bones, Shadow could feel the malicious nature of whoever had made these prints. The same feeling he'd had looking into the grotto where Caitlin Bledsoe's killer had hidden.

Shadow took the radio from his belt and raised it to his face.

"23 to 1"

"Go ahead, 23."

"Chief, I found something, but. . ." He hesitated. If Martin was still standing by the parents, his report would really upset them. "Sir, are we on a secure channel?"

"Of course we're not, Fletcher. Every ranger in the park can... Oh, I see what you mean. I'm alone. Go ahead. What do you have?"

"I found fresh tracks, sir. But they're not from a kid. It's an adult, heading northwest, away from the campgrounds. I'm just north of Campground B."

Shadow didn't mention the tracks were those of a barefoot man. It was weird, but it didn't make any difference as far as the kid was concerned."

"Okay, stay there. I'll be right there."

Shadow quickly keyed his mike. "Sir, I'm over half a mile from you. I need to get on this trail right away. If there is a connection with the missing boy, time is crucial."

"You're right, Fletcher. You and Goodluck follow those tracks. We'll be right behind you."

"10-4"

Shadow considered whether to wait for Jack. It might be several minutes. He took out his automatic pistol, chambered a round, and set off along the trail. Knowing that it would probably get him into trouble, he turned off the radio so there'd be no unexpected transmission to give him away.

The barefoot man had a stride a bit longer than Shadow, so he wasn't much taller; he just had huge feet in proportion to his body. And he wasn't very heavy, either. Shadow could tell by how hard the snow was packed. That made him feel a bit more hopeful, since the weight of a carried child would be reflected in the tracks. This situation was getting stranger and stranger. Why would someone walk through snow barefooted?

But the main thing was that the man in front of Shadow was walking leisurely. It meant Shadow had a chance. He began to run. The snow wasn't very deep, but he still had to be careful not to slip, so he couldn't run at full speed. With every step, the foul aura seemed to grow and his urgency increased apace.

He came to the edge of the flat area and looked down a rugged slope, dotted with large boulders and rock formations. Far below was Grassy Creek, running through a palette of colors, the autumn leaves just past their peak of beauty and beginning to fall from the branches. He got lucky. He spied the speck of someone was crossing the shallow water, carrying a blue bundle over his shoulder that just possibly could be a child. Shadow watched for a few seconds. Whoever was down there looked impossibly thin, but then again he was observing from on high, at a steep angle.

Didn't matter. Even though he wasn't far away, Shadow was almost an hour behind his quarry, because it would be slow going over this rough ground. But, then again, the kidnapper had stayed on the trails. Shadow would have to cut across country to gain time. He studied the slope below him. It looked like there might be a trail, of sorts. It was nothing like the trails maintained for the tourists, obviously made by wild animals, deer probably.

Shadow started down, gaining ground quickly, letting gravity do most of the work. Without warning, the light snow slipped under his weight and he went down. Feet first, he went down the steep slope, faster and faster as inertia and gravity took relentless hold. All he could do was to dig his heels in and keep his head up to avoid being knocked senseless by the many rocks that were bruising his buttocks and back. He saw a large boulder below him and braced for the impact.

Luckily, he was able to absorb most of the shock with his legs, but it still hurt. For a few seconds, he lay still, gathering his wits. His legs—hell, his whole body was sore, but he didn't feel like anything was broken. He forced himself up and continued on.

Trouble was, he was off the trail now and the going was tougher. He finally reached the bottom and came out on the bank of Grassy Creek. He couldn't be sure, but he'd probably come down a couple of hundred yards from where he had seen the kidnapper. Shadow wanted to stay directly behind him, since there would probably be a trail he was following. Whoever this guy was, he knew the territory.

Sure enough, he found the trail right where he expected it and resumed the pursuit through the trees. There was a clear trail, again narrow, but what Shadow had expected. There were no clear footprints to be found here, where little snow had reached the ground. He was sure he was following his prey, though. All he needed were the few branches broken off by a man carrying a burden and shallow impressions in soft soil to tell he was gaining rapidly. The ground wasn't level—about the only level areas in the park were the man-made parking lots and campgrounds—but the going wasn't rough.

He came out of the trees, into a rocky area, probably the result of a landslide that had carried trees away, years ago. Huge boulders, taller than a man, stood like sentries. He'd have to weave between them to get through. Here, most of the snowfall had melted, but there were still patches where it had drifted up against boulders. There was no trail here; he would have to call on all his tracking abilities to follow the kidnapper through the maze.

Surprisingly, Shadow found prints here and there, where the barefoot traveler hadn't bothered to avoid leaving clues. He must be confident that no one was after him. After a few more minutes he could see trees ahead. He'd soon be out of the slide area and have a solid trail to follow again.

Then he heard something ahead—a child, weeping. He picked up the pace and the sound grew. Coming around a large boulder, he almost stumbled over the little boy lying at the base of it, with his hands over his face. The child wore a blue snowsuit with black boots and Shadow was sure it had to be Mark Kaminski. He could feel the frigid malevolence that he'd felt before, emanating from the boy.

Grandma Min's charm seemed to be vibrating against his chest. He looked about. No one. Why had the kidnapper dropped the child here? Maybe he. . .

Shadow sensed a shadow above him and realized the vile aura came not from little Mark but from up there, atop the boulder. He began to look up, but then something hard slammed into his forehead with enough force to knock him backward. Just as when he'd been shot, the back of his head landed on a smooth rock, jarring him into a stunned state.

He tried to move, but couldn't. His ears were filled with a ringing buzz that kept him from hearing anything else. Sensing movement close by, he managed to open his eyes. A pair of long, emaciated legs loomed in his vision. Then, closer to him, a pair of incredibly skinny arms came from somewhere above and soundlessly took hold of little Mark. The bare arms were covered by patches of clear, dead skin, like someone might have as sunburn blisters sloughed off. Shadow's nostrils were filled with the putrid stench of decaying flesh, the same foul odor he'd sensed in the alcove where Caitlin Bledsoe's abductor had hidden.

Elongated, bony fingers took hold of the boy's blue jumpsuit and hoisted him up. Shadow tried to follow with his eyes, but his brain didn't feel like moving his eyeballs at the moment.

The legs began quickly moving away from him and, without Shadow moving his eyes, more and more of the kidnapper came into view. It was human, but yet it wasn't. Several inches over six feet tall, it was an incredibly skinny—almost skeletal—figure. The bumps along its spine were prominent, as well as its ribs. The thing appeared to be silver because skin was sloughing off the entire gray-skinned body. There was none of the healthy glow of living human skin; it looked more like a corpse. There was no hint of hair on the back of the skull-like head. It was naked, with emaciated buttocks. Little Mark Kaminski was slung over a shoulder, like a haunch of venison.

The thing—although it looked like a man, Shadow knew better—went around a boulder and was lost from sight. Shadow stared out at the scene and wondered why he couldn't move. Was his neck broken?

CHAPTER TWENTY-FOUR

"DO YOU KNOW HOW CRAZY THIS ALL IS?"

After a time that felt like an eternity because he couldn't go after the boy, Shadow's feeling returned. He was able to blink his eyes. It was a good sign, but it brought an intense, pounding headache into his awareness.

He began moving his fingers, trying to speed his recovery. In a few minutes, he was able to sit up. His first thought was to call for help on the radio, but it wasn't on his belt. He found it nearby, smashed. The creature must have pulled it from its case without Shadow feeling. He staggered to his feet and stumbled back into the chase, sliding the useless radio into its case. He'd been a ranger too long to leave it behind as litter.

There wasn't much hope, he knew. He wasn't moving very quickly and it was obvious that his quarry was taking long strides, nearly running. From here on, Shadow wouldn't have the advantage of the creature being unaware it was being followed.

Feeling a cool breeze on his forehead, he put a hand to where he'd been hit. The hand came away bloody. He'd been hit with a rock, no doubt, or the hilt of a knife. How the hell had the thing known it was being trailed? Had Shadow made that much noise when he slid down the slope?

About three-quarters of an hour later, he sensed someone coming up behind him. A glance over his shoulder revealed Shawnee Jack, gaining rapidly on him.

Shadow was glad to see the other ranger. He was breathing like a bellows, clouds of steam coming from his mouth, not sure he'd be able to keep up the chase much longer, He decided to stop and catch his breath so he could fill Jack in on the situation.

Soon Jack was with him. He was breathing hard, but naturally. Shadow could tell he had a lot of staying power left.

"Good to see you," Shadow said, puffing.

131

"I'll bet. You look like you got sucker-punched."

Shadow nodded and pointed ahead. "It's got the boy."

Jacks eyebrows arched. "It?"

"I don't know what it was." Shadow shook his head, trying to clear it. "It looked like a man, sort of. More like a skeleton, really. And it can move really fast."

The other man's eyes went even wider and a look of fear came over his face. "Wendigo!" he whispered, as though speaking to himself.

"What?"

"I'll tell you later. There's no time to waste."

Jack took off on the trail. It was still fairly easy to follow, but the snow was melting away fast. The creature could easily disappear into the mountains if Jack didn't catch it soon, Shadow knew.

Shadow was left to decide. Should he continue on after Jack, or go back to meet the other rangers who must be following? It didn't take much thought. Even if he couldn't keep up, he needed to follow on, just in case he might be of some help to Jack. The boy deserved it.

*

When the sun went behind the mountains, leaving him in gloom, Shadow knew he had to go back. He'd lost the trail hours ago and searched randomly now, hoping for blind luck. But he had to go back. He had eaten a candy bar from his pocket this afternoon, but now had no food or water, nothing to light a fire and it would soon grow bitterly cold. If he stayed on the mountainside through the night, he might need rescue himself.

It was uphill going and it was nearly full dark by the time he got back up to the main part of the park. Campers and rangers still milled around the area, but most of the RV's were gone. Parents didn't want their kids to stay where a child had just been abducted.

He asked around, but none of the other rangers had seen Jack since the morning, so he must still be out there. Shadow got back in his truck and drove to the park office.

Doris had gone home long since, apparently, because a ranger sat at her desk.

"Hey, Bill," Shadow said. "I just got back and need to check in with the chief."

"Any luck?"

Shadow, weary, wanted to say he would have mentioned it immediately if he'd found the boy, but didn't.

"No, where's the chief?"

"He's on his way back here. He should be just a few minutes. There's coffee in the conference room. What happened to your forehead?"

Without answering Shadow stepped into the conference room. There was not only coffee, but sodas, sandwiches, crackers, cookies, and the like. He popped open a soda and chugged it, then began munching on cookies, hoping for an energy boost from the sugar and caffeine. Too bad someone hadn't thought to lay out a few Snickers bars.

He heard a commotion out in the office and then Chief Martin barged into the conference room. His eyes went to Shadow's forehead then came down to stare at his face.

"Fletcher! Where the hell have you been?"

Taken aback, Shadow said, "Out looking for the missing boy, where the hell do you think I've been?"

"Why didn't you check in? Goodluck radioed that he'd passed you on the trail and you'd been hurt."

"Oh." Shadow backed down. "My radio got broke."

Martin looked as though he was about to say, *"That's a likely story,"* but he didn't.

"Well, we've been calling for hours." He was still blustering, but it came out lame. "What happened to your head?"

Shadow took a deep breath. It was hard to admit he'd been outwitted in the outdoors.

"The kidnapper, whoever he was, got on top of a boulder and hit me with a rock or something. It knocked me silly for a while."

"Can you describe him?"

Shadow shook his head. "I never even got a look at him."

"Then how do you know it was the kidnapper?"

"I saw the boy. The, uh. . . guy set the kid out in the open to distract me while he bushwhacked me."

"The boy was alive?" Martin asked.

"Yeah. He was crying."

"But you never saw who took him?"

"No."

Martin wearily sighed. "Okay, that's enough for now. I'll get the details from you later. You go home and get some sleep. We'll take up the search tomorrow, and I want a complete report from you as soon as you clock in tomorrow." He pulled a styrofoam cup from a stack.

"Is there any word of Ranger Goodluck?" Shadow asked.

Martin gave a curt nod as he filled his cup with coffee. "Yeah, he came out on the highway down in Kentucky. I sent someone down to give him a lift home."

"Good." Shadow began to leave the room but then turned back to face his boss.

"One other thing."

"What?" Martin sipped from his cup.

"Did you and the other rangers follow me and Jack's trail?"

Martin nodded. "Of course."

"Did anyone notice anything odd about the footprints?"

"No, they were melted all soft and gooey around the edges by then. It just looked like several people following one another. Why?"

Shadow shrugged. "Oh, nothing. Just that some of the other rangers might have picked up something I missed." He turned and left the room before Martin could ask any more questions.

"And get somebody to take a look at your forehead," Martin called after him.

*

Half an hour later, as he'd expected, Shadow heard tapping on his back door. A moment later, Shawnee Jack came into the kitchen, carrying a bottle of Jack Daniels.

"We need to talk," he said. "You got any Cokes?"

Shadow, sitting at the kitchen table, having a bowl of Froot Loops and a beer, nodded. "In the fridge. Open me another beer while you're in there, would you?"

It had become habit for Jack to open Shadow's beer when they were together. Shadow could get a can open, if he had to, but usually spilled some.

Jack took a glass from the wire rack in the sink and poured a generous shot of whiskey into it, then added a couple of ice cubes from the freezer. He opened the refrigerator and took a beer and a coke from it. Holding the cans in one hand and his unfinished drink in the other, he joined Shadow at the table. He opened both cans, slid the beer over to Shadow, then added coke to the glass.

"We need to talk." He took a large drink.

Shadow nodded. "You said that already."

Jack returned the nod. "You saw the tracks."

"Big son of a bitch, walking barefoot, missing the two outer toes on the left foot."

Jack took another drink. "What do you make of it?"

"I have no idea what to think," Shadow admitted. "Especially now that I saw. . . whatever I saw."

"I'm going to tell you a story."

"Shoot," said Shadow.

Jack held up a finger. "Wait, I need another drink for this." He swallowed the remainder in his glass and went to the counter for the whiskey bottle and into the fridge for a coke. Returning to his chair, he made another drink and took a sip from it. He straightened, took a deep breath and then looked directly into Shadow's eyes.

"Remember I told you about my brother, David, him going up to Alaska and all?"

Shadow gave a brief nod.

"Well, he liked it up there," Jack continued. "He'd send me a letter every six months or so. Seems the second winter he was there, he got caught out in some bad weather and got frostbit. He lost two toes off his left foot."

"Holy shit," Shadow murmured.

Jack nodded solemnly and took a drink.

"That ain't the half of it," he said.

"What do you mean?"

Shadow's mind was reeling. No wonder Jack had seemed worried. He had known his brother was somehow involved in this.

Jack continued. "Two years later, him and two other prospectors got snowed

134

into a remote pass for the entire winter. When rescuers found them in the spring, they found the bones of two men. They never found hide nor hair of Davey."

"What do you mean?"

Jack took another drink.

"Just what I said. He's never been heard from since. And that was three years ago."

Shadow's mind raced. If Jack's brother had made those tracks, what was that creature he'd seen?

"But...but...now you know he's alive, right. I mean...we saw his tracks. Aren't you sure that was your brother?"

Jack snorted and grimaced. "I wish."

"What do you mean?" Shadow realized he was now the one repeating things.

"You got hit in the head. Did you see who hit you?"

"Yes, but I don't know whether I can believe what I saw. I was pretty groggy."

Jack got up and brought two more cans to the table. He opened a beer and slid it over to Shadow, who realized he hadn't touched the first beer. He picked it up and sipped as Jack made a second drink, even stronger than the first two.

He needed to wait Jack out. Jack had told so many old stories and legends that he tended to be melodramatic.

"Tell me what you saw," Jack said.

Shadow described the creature he'd seen, while Jack nodded.

"That seems to fit the bill."

"What do you. . .?" Shadow stopped himself.

"There's an old Indian legend from the north," Jack began.

Shadow cut him off. "Oh, come on, Jack. You mean you've been leading up to another one of your old..."

Jack held up a finger. "Hear me out. It's not uncommon up in that frozen country to get snowed in, the way David did. The way they tell it, sometimes it comes down to cannibalism to survive, like the Donner party out west. . ."

Shadow felt himself nodding.

"They say that if someone resorts to cannibalism to survive, he or she is cursed. If they survive and return to civilization, they'll be reviled and shunned. But if they don't..."

Jack paused dramatically and Shadow waited him out.

"If they don't, if they freeze or starve to death, they turn into an immortal ice creature. They're dead, like in the zombie movies, but they still move around. And not like in the movies, either. They're fast and wily and strong as all-get-out. And they don't want to eat just your brains; that would only be an appetizer. They want to eat every bit of your flesh."

"Come on, Jack. . ."

"No, hear me out. My brother died up there in Alaska and he turned into the popsicle version of a zombie. It took three years, on foot, but he's finally come home. But it's not really him, anymore, is it?"

Shadow thumped The Claw on the table. "Knock it off, Jack. Do you know how crazy this all is?"

Jack leaned forward and glared. "I sure do, buddy. But I found a three-toed track in the snow last winter, a couple of months before that first girl was taken. And don't you think I'd know my brother's track, even without the missing toes? Hell, it doesn't matter if he was barefoot or not, I'd know him by his stride, by how he puts his feet down. It was my brother. But my brother's dead."

Shadow wet his lips, which had suddenly gone dry. He picked up his beer and sipped while he wondered what to believe. His common sense told him that old legends were a bunch of bullshit, but his senses told him he'd seen the track of a monster and then seen the monster itself.

Finally, he said, "And you say these things are immortal?"

Jack nodded. His drink was gone and he poured more whiskey into the glass without bothering with Coke. He sipped it.

"That's what they say. The only way to kill it is to melt it down to its core, so I guess you'd have to throw it into a fire or something."

"And what do they call this zombie-creature?" asked Shadow.

"A wendigo."

CHAPTER TWENTY-FIVE

"YOU EXAMINED THE REMAINS?"

The next morning, Shadow not only had to write his report, he was interviewed by Sergeant Bednarski and Agent Langley, both sitting across the conference table from him. He stuck to his story of not seeing his attacker and neglected to mention the barefoot tracks. He still wasn't quite sure what had happened between him and Bednarski at the hospital, but knew he wouldn't be believed about the latest events. Hell, would *he* believe it if someone told him about a zombie?

When they were through questioning him, Shadow decided to ask a few questions of his own.

"What's with the guy in the paper yesterday, the one they arrested in West Virginia?" he asked Langley, who would be more likely to share information.

"What about him?" Langley said disingenuously.

"I mean, if he was the suspect in both the other cases, he couldn't have done it again yesterday."

"What makes you think we're looking at him for both cases?" Langley asked, drinking coffee from a Styrofoam cup.

"And what business is it of yours, anyway?" Bednarski added.

"Easy, Sergeant," said Langley. "I think Fletcher knows something we don't. Remember, we haven't had a chance to look into yesterday's abduction yet. Maybe if we're frank with him, he would be inclined to be more forthcoming." He raised an eyebrow at Shadow.

"What makes you think I know something?" Shadow asked.

A smile twitched at Langley's mouth. "I've interviewed a lot of people. You get a feeling."

"All right, I'll tell you this much. I don't think he could have had anything to do with the first case, much less this one. The two abductions from the park were

137

done by one individual, in the wilderness, and carried deeper into the hills. The girl taken in the summer was in a park almost downtown and was taken out of state in a vehicle. So you're looking for someone else, probably with a connection to The Breaks."

Langley nodded. "That's the way I'm thinking. Of course, with only two cases and the second not investigated yet, it's too soon to start profiling." He sipped from his cup.

"And you're not looking for a pedophile, either, are you? Not in the regular way, I mean."

The F.B.I. man's eyes narrowed. "What are you talking about?"

"The knife marks on that little girl's bones, that's what I'm talking about. She was dismembered but not scattered to hide the evidence, so why was she cut to pieces?"

Bednarski couldn't keep quiet any longer. He rose in his chair. "You examined the remains? I told you to keep your damned nose out of my case."

Langley held up a hand. "Hold on there, Sergeant. The Bledsoe girl was taken from Virginia and found in Kentucky. That makes it my case. I'm just letting you in on it out of professional courtesy."

The police sergeant didn't turn toward Langley, but sat down slowly, glaring at Shadow, visibly fighting his urge to speak. Shadow met his gaze, keeping his own face expressionless.

"The way I figure it, somebody cut that girl into pieces. He butchered her like a hog."

Bednarski's face was going beet red.

"Some son of a bitch," Shadow continued, his eyes challenging the sergeant. "ate that little girl. That same somebody kept returning there and feeding on her until the meat was too spoiled, then left her for the animals and insects to clean the bones. Is that the way you figure it, Agent Langley." Shadow turned to the F.B.I. man.

"Not quite," Langley replied. "It's obvious that she was hacked apart, but it could have just been some sort of mutilation. Of course, cannibalism was considered but it's so rare, we're not going down that road. Not yet, at least. Unless you know something we don't."

Shadow shook his head. "Just a feeling. Like when I felt something was wrong when everyone else still assumed the Bledsoe girl was only lost."

It was the truth, too. He'd had a strong hunch cannibalism was involved when he examined the remains. Shawnee Jack's recent story of wendigos only confirmed his suspicions.

Langley shook his head. "You and your feelings."

He drank the last gulp of coffee and pitched the cup into the trash.

Shadow went back to writing his report, using The Claw to hold the pen. With his right hand, he rubbed lightly over the bandage compress Jack had stuck over his forehead injury. Not only did the wound itch, but there was a pounding headache behind it.

WENDIGO

He heard a helicopter fly past overhead and concluded an aerial search had begun. He doubted it would do them any good; the wendigo would go to cover in a cave. Would it know to hide from a helicopter? When a person turned into a zombie, did anything of their personality or thought process carry over? Since this wendigo had traveled for thousands of miles of open country to return to the home of the man it had been, it seemed likely.

He shoved the paperwork away and got up. He needed some fresh air. Since there were no windows in the conference room, he went through the outer office and onto the porch. That was no good, either; the stench from the restaurant's dumpsters drove him to walk down the path along the top of the escarpment. The Breaks plummeted down on his left, but he was nowhere near the edge.

He walked along the well-defined path that allowed visitors staying in the scenic cabins to walk to the lodge for their meals. A chipmunk scurried across in front of him, but he paid it no mind. When he'd first arrived at the park, he'd never seen a chipmunk before and thought they were cute. They still were, but there were so damned many of them near the cabins, where they could scavenge for tourist scraps, that he didn't even notice them anymore.

Could he really have just asked himself about zombie behavior like they were real? He wondered if he might be losing his mind. Yet he had seen a man-like creature yesterday, and couldn't deny his memory. True, he'd been a bit woozy from getting hit, but he knew what he'd seen. Nevertheless, could it possibly be the wendigo of legend?

*

Shadow and Shawnee Jack got together later in the morning and managed to convince the chief ranger that they should search the area in Kentucky where they'd found the remains of the Bledsoe girl. Martin agreed so readily that Shadow wondered if he was being gotten rid of. Well, it wouldn't hurt his feelings any; he wasn't too fond of Martin, either.

Over the next few days, the two rangers didn't hunt for the boy, really. They searched for small, out-of-the-way caves and grottoes that might conceal his body. This time, Shadow's body and lungs were accustomed to the thin mountain air and he managed to keep up. He kept his pockets filled with candy bars and other sweets to fuel his exertions.

In the evenings, they would discuss the situation over beer and bourbon. Jack had studied the subject of wendigos for quite a while now and said he had a pretty good idea of what they were up against, even though all the evidence was hearsay or fable.

The wendigo seemed to have started as part of the traditional belief systems of various Algonquian-speaking tribes in the northern United States and Canada, like the Ojibwe, the Iroquois, and the Cree. The wendigo were insatiable cannibals who remained emaciated, even though they gorged themselves when they found a victim.

There was no defense against a wendigo, but some tribes had performed a dance during times of famine to re-enforce the taboo against cannibalism to

139

protect against anyone "going wendigo."

There was also a condition known as "Wendigo Psychosis," when a Native American of a northern tribe believed he had become a Wendigo and was attracted to cannibalism even when other food was available. If the tribe's shamans couldn't cure one of these unfortunates, they were executed by the tribe. There were documented cases of this psychosis, and not that long ago.

One such person, a Cree man named Swift Runner, had famously butchered and eaten his wife and several children in 1878, despite being only twenty-five miles from a Hudson Bay Company's supply post. In 1907, an Oji-Cree man named Jack Fiddler and his brother had been arrested for killing fourteen people they claimed to be wendigos.

If anyone—Chief Ranger Martin, for example—ever found out that Shadow and Jack were discussing a mythical monster as being real, that person would probably consider them deranged. But Shadow had grown up with Grandma Min and been exposed to Native American mysticism, so he knew that some aspects of the ancient legends seemed to be true—at least to someone with aboriginal blood. As an adult, he had nearly forgotten about his earlier experiences since nothing supernatural ever occurred to or around him while he'd been stationed around the country and the world. It was only after he'd returned to his native land of Virginia that he'd become aware of anything that smacked of mysticism. Or maybe it was because he'd been knocked silly by the bomb that had taken his hand.

He considered asking Jack about his background, but it just wasn't the sort of question men could ask of each other. Was that some of the "stoic Indian" stereotype? No matter, he could tell that Jack was as much of a believer in the supernatural as he was.

After a few days, the search was called off. The two Native American rangers continued to hunt, however, even though the kidnapped boy was surely dead by know. Instead, the looked for a clue that would lead them to the wendigo. Jack carried a rifle along, since they had decided it had to be stopped. Otherwise, the wendigo would be back for another meal.

Then, one morning when they were off-duty and had planned to search, Shadow awoke to a world of white. The accumulation of overnight snowfall was too deep for them to search, he knew. Even a strong, fit man would be unable to negotiate this rugged country fighting against knee-to-hip-deep snow. Even a wendigo, supposedly supernaturally strong, would have trouble getting around. Or would it? It was a creature of the far north, maybe it wasn't slowed by deep snow.

Which reminded Shadow how quickly the creature had traveled, even though it had no way of knowing it was being pursued. If the wendigo had known, Shadow would have been left far behind. Even if he and Jack sighted it on one of their searches, they'd never get near enough for a rifle shot.

That evening, as the two rangers drank and played cribbage, Shadow mentioned his concern.

Jack puffed air between his lips in dismissal. "Don't really matter, does it? This snow will stay until spring. We'll just have to wait until then."

"But it might take another kid before spring," Shadow said. "And then it might just lay low during the summer, since it only seems to come out when there's snow on the ground."

"Can't do anything about that." Jack sipped his whiskey.

"Maybe we can."

"What do you mean?"

Shadow drew up his chair. "Have you ever used snowshoes?"

Jack's eyebrows rose. "I'm a Shawnee, not an Eskimo." Then he looked thoughtful. "I wonder if they still sell those things."

John Bushore

CHAPTER TWENTY-SIX

"DO YOU NEED ANY HELP?"

"God, Dad, how can you stand it? I'm about to go out of my freakin' mind with boredom and I've only been here a couple of days."

Shadow winced at her language, but let it go. He'd have to get used to the fact that Ashley was growing up.

"It's not so bad," he said. "I was thinking that tomorrow we can take a Christmas Eve walk along some of the easier trails and enjoy the scenery. Even though the lodge is open, not many tourists come up here over the holidays and they stay inside. We'll have the place to ourselves."

He'd been nervous ever since Ashley had arrived. Although there'd been no sign of the wendigo, or anything else out of the ordinary, he sensed it was nearby—or maybe it was just fatherly concern.

"You're kidding, right?" Ashley said. "You actually expect me to go out in this snow? It must be a foot deep."

"Sure. It'll be fun. If nothing else, we'll walk along the road."

"Yeah, right."

"No, really," he said. "We can. . ."

He stopped talking because Ashley's phone was signaling an incoming text message. He'd learned that she would drop whatever she was doing and text her reply, oblivious to everything except her phone. The entire rangers' quarters was wired as an internet hot spot and she could not only phone and text here, atop the mountain, but she could access the internet. If not, she'd have been even more bored.

Yesterday, her first day with him, she'd been all excited about being in the park, sending photos of the mountains to her friends. But now the novelty of the place had worn off, and she had grown bored.

When she'd finished and put her phone down, he asked, "So what do you do all day in Richmond when you're at home?"

She shrugged. "Hang out in my room, text my friends, stuff like that."

Pretty much the same things she was doing here. He stifled a sigh. "You want to watch TV?"

He'd bought a small, flat-screen set to put in her room, since she'd complained about watching TV out in the living room last August. It hadn't impressed her. She was more concerned that she would be sharing the bathroom with him, even though it had not been a problem for her the last time she'd visited.

"I don't know," she said. "When will your girlfriend get here?"

"Soon. She'll call once she gets checked into the lodge. And she's just a friend."

"Whatever."

Xan had called him in early December and asked if he would like to have her spend the holiday with him. He'd been surprised she was still interested in him, now that he'd ditched Min's love charm, and so pleased he'd agreed immediately. Then he'd remembered Ashley would be staying with him and backtracked, asking Xan if she'd mind staying in the lodge. She'd understood.

After he'd hung up, he realized this would be a great arrangement. The house was small and there'd be no privacy for the two of them with Ashley in the next bedroom.

The phone on the kitchen wall rang and Xan announced she was checked in. They'd agreed to have dinner at the Rhododendron Restaurant on the first evening, for she and Ashley to become acquainted, so Shadow said they'd be over at seven p.m.

When he'd hung up, Ashley made a surprising suggestion, something Shadow thought was well beyond her years.

"Seven is hours away. Why don't you go over and help your friend get settled in? I think I'm going to take a long, hot bath, anyway. You can come back and pick me up for dinner."

He hesitated. "I don't want to leave you alone."

She frowned and whined. "Daaaad, I'm not a little kid, you know. I'll be fine."

Again he wavered. He hadn't told her about the two abducted children and *certainly* hadn't mentioned anything called a wendigo.

"All right," he finally said. "But you have to promise to stay in the house while I'm gone."

Her sigh was as dramatic as that of any stage actress. "Why would I go outside—to build a snowman? I told you, Dad, I'm a big girl now, nearly a woman, and you need to lighten up."

He tried to suppress a grin, but knew he failed. "Okay, okay. It's just that you don't know the area and, if it starts snowing, you could get lost within yards of the house."

Then he had another thought, something he might scare her with, to keep her indoors. "And don't forget there are bears in these mountains."

144

Would Ashley remember that bears hibernated in winter?

Apparently not, because she said, "Dad, I told you, I'm going to take a hot bath. Why do you keep this place so cold, anyway?"

"Okay, turn up the thermostat then. Just don't turn the place into a sauna, all right?"

Ashley's mention of the hot bath reminded him that he could do with a shower before meeting Xan. But maybe that would work in his favor; he and Xan were close enough that she wouldn't mind washing his back—or more—in the room's shower.

*

"We're here, Ashley," Shadow yelled as he closed the door behind him and Xan. "Come and meet Xan."

He noticed that it was hot in the house, eighty degrees or more. His daughter had obviously turned the thermostat way up. Luckily, he didn't pay for heat, but it still annoyed him. He went to the wall and turned the heat down. He noticed that the door to her room and door to the bathroom were both closed.

"Ashley," he called again. "Come on out."

"Maybe she's texting," he said to Xan. "She's oblivious to anything when she texts. You could set off a firecracker next to her ear and she probably wouldn't notice."

He went to the door and knocked. "Ashley, are you in there?"

No response.

"I'm coming in. Are you decent?" He knocked hard on the door again. "Hey!"

When she still didn't answer, he turned the knob and opened the door slowly, ready to pull it shut if he saw something he shouldn't. Jesus, he'd be up in front of the judge again.

But Ashley wasn't in the room. He went to the bathroom door and rapped loudly. "Ashley, are you in there?"

No response here, either. He knocked hard enough to rattle the door.

"Ashley, answer me."

"Ashley, honey, are you all right in there?" Xan said, stepping up next to him. "Do you need any help?"

No answer came, so Shadow tried the knob. Locked. She was either unconscious in there or—and he felt a knot in his stomach—she wasn't in the house. No, the door was locked, so she must be inside. With a glance at Xan, who looked worried, he reached up and felt along the top of the door frame with his good hand until he found the long, wire-like key that would release the lock from the outside. He kicked the bottom of the door, to make more noise than knocking would produce.

"Ashley, I'm coming in."

He felt the lock turn, and began to open the door, but hesitated. He turned to Xan. "You'd better check."

She slipped inside and, a second later, he heard a piercing scream. Water sloshed and Xan backed out of the bathroom.

145

"Is she okay?" he asked, although he was sure Ashley was all right if she could scream."

Xan rolled her eyes and shook her head, but she was holding back laughter. "She's okay."

"Why didn't she answer?"

From inside the bathroom, he heard Ashley cursing, using words he hadn't even known at her age.

"She was in the tub with earphones, listening to her I-Pod and texting on her phone at the same time."

"So why is she swearing?"

"She dropped her phone into the water." Xan tried to hold back a giggle, but failed. "Kids!" She shrugged.

He tried to reason with Ashley after she'd stormed to her room, wrapped in a towel, to emerge clothed and angry. She blamed Shadow and Xan for the loss of her "smart phone," whatever that was. He had assumed it was just an ordinary phone.

"We wouldn't have bothered you if you'd answered," he said. "And you shouldn't use electronic devices when you're in the water?"

"Whatever!" her eyes rose toward the ceiling. "I told you I was going to take a hot bath; you should have known."

"But that was hours ago. How could you stay in the tub so long?"

"This house is freezing," she answered in an icy voice. "Every time the water got cold, I let it out and added more hot."

"Why were you wasting so much energy?"

"I told you. I was cold. And I was bored. There's nothing to do around here."

"How would you know? You haven't stopped texting since you got here."

She'd cocked her head and gave him an evil, sarcastic smile. "Well, I won't be texting anymore, now, will I?"

CHAPTER TWENTY-SEVEN

"WHAT SAY WE GO FOR A WALK?"

Christmas Eve began with a steady snowfall, adding to the snow already on the ground. Ashley seemed to be in a better mood, snarling only occasionally. The two of them circled around each other in the small house like a pair of wild animals in a cage. She mostly watched TV—while listening to her MP3, which he'd learned was a device to download music—as Shadow shined his shoes and cleaned his service revolver. He also oiled the rifle he'd purchased, a Winchester .308 with a scope.

"That's a good choice," Jack had said. "A three-oh-eight will bring down anything you'll find down in the lower forty-eight, 'cept maybe a moose."

"I think our friend out there came from a little farther north," Shadow had answered. "Not to mention you said he's immortal."

When he'd run out of makeshift things to do, he went up to Ashley, who was watching TV with her earphones on. Shadow wasn't sure if she was watching or listening to music. He gestured for her to take off the earphones.

"What say we go for a walk? Stretch our legs a bit before Xan comes over for lunch."

"Do we have to?" she whined. "I was hoping you could take me down to town so I could get a new I-Phone."

"I thought it was a "smart" phone."

"Same thing, Dad."

"I don't know," he said. "How much do those things cost?"

She shrugged. "You don't have to worry about money. It was insured and I already used your phone to call and set up a new one. Normally, I'd have them ship it to me, but it'll be quicker to pick it up at one of their stores. They're open late on Christmas Eve; I checked."

He shook his head. "I'm sure you did. But I'll call the park office and check how the roads are."

"Why?"

"Ashley, we're on top of a mountain. The roads might not be cleared. It's nearly impossible to go up the side of a mountain on a slick road and it's suicidal to go down."

Her face fell. "You're just making excuses."

"No, I'm not. If the plows have cleared the way, I'll take you to town. You sure that your phone company has a branch there?"

"I'm sure." Her face brightened.

"Okay, then, let's go for a walk and I'll check on the roads after lunch. Would you mind if Xan went with us?"

She shrugged. "Nope. Suit yourself."

"Put on something warm, then, and let's take that walk. Wear your boots."

He slipped his service weapon, a 9mm Sig Sauer, into a pocket of his heavy jacket, being careful not to let her see. He didn't want to have to explain his need for a pistol.

There was nearly a foot of snow on the ground, so they had to slog through it until they reached the road, which had been cleared by the park's plow earlier, leaving a long mound of snow on one side of the road. It reminded Shadow that he needed to take time to try out the new snowshoes he'd purchased along with the rifle. Jack had also gotten a pair. They planned to be ready if—when—the wendigo struck again.

The snow drifted down in flat, lazy flakes. There was little wind, so the cold air was quite pleasant. The only sound came from the crunching of their boots in the inch or so of snow on the asphalt roadway.

There were no tracks of man, animal, or vehicle to be seen, only a rolling landscape of snow. The dark branches of the trees were topped by a decorative accumulation of white. The only sign of life was smoke coming from the chimneys of the other rangers' homes adding the tang of woodsmoke to the air.

"This is beautiful," Ashley said, her cheeks rosy from the cold. "We hardly ever get snow in Richmond and never anything like this."

"Don't I know it?"

Shadow wasn't used to such snowfall, either, having grown up on the coast of Virginia, where hurricanes were more common than heavy snowstorms. Now that he was in Breaks Park for the winter, he was beginning to wonder if it had been wise to accept the transfer here. What was it going to be like when winter really set in?

Shadow suddenly was awash with that strange awareness of evil that he'd developed, coming from behind. He stopped and whirled. The wendigo! It would come out onto the road between them and his house and was moving too fast to get around it.

"Jesus H. Christ," he cursed. Why hadn't he felt its presence before now? It must have been right behind his house when they'd come out the front door.

He sensed Ashley turning next to him and heard her scream as she caught sight of the naked, decaying monstrosity rushing toward them.

"Get behind me," he said, reaching into his pocket and beginning to withdraw his pistol.

But Ashley didn't just get behind him; she threw her arms around him and screamed in his ear. She grabbed and clutched at him as if she were trying to climb him.

The gun hung up on the pocket lining. He tried to use The Claw to hold the jacket steady, but it was impossible with Ashley clutching at his every move.

"Ashley, let go," he yelled above her screaming.

He tugged mightily at the gun and, with a ripping sound, it came free. Then it came out of his grasp, falling onto the snow-covered roadway in front of him.

The wendigo had reached the road and was sprinting toward them. Goddamnit, why couldn't it be a regular, shuffling, slow zombie instead of this hyped up monster?

"Ashley, for God's sake, let go of me." He fell to his knees, taking her with him.

He got a hand on the gun and managed to pick it up. But until he could jack the slide back and chamber a round, it was a useless hunk of metal. And that was always tricky with one hand and a prosthesis. Glancing up, he saw the wendigo rushing toward him.

He couldn't look at the creature, though; his eyes were needed to guide the nerveless claw to grab the slide. The gun was slippery in his left hand, so he knew there wouldn't be much friction, which was what he normally counted on.

Ashley was still all over him, but he'd forgotten about her, in a way. Her clutching hands had become part of a universe of impediments to getting the gun ready. Her screaming was dwarfed by the caterwauling of his instincts to survive the aura of evil that was invading his inner soul.

This was far worse than any combat situation he'd ever been in. It wasn't the wendigo or *him*, it was the wendigo or Ashley.

Trembling, he managed to chamber a round. He'd been in too many battles to forget the safety. He clicked it off and, still on his knees, raised the gun with his right—and only—hand. All he had to do now was pull the trigger. He wasn't as good a shot with his remaining hand, since he'd originally been left handed, but he did okay on the range.

The attacking wendigo was only twenty feet away, coming on fast. Shadow aimed, the gun jerking around as Ashley pulled at him. The instant the sights crossed the creature's chest, he squeezed the trigger. Not the best shot he'd ever made, because the wendigo didn't slow a bit.

It was only ten feet away when he got off another shot and this time he saw putrefied flesh disintegrate as the bullet hit high, just below the throat. The bullet went right on through, apparently, because Shadow could see that paper-like debris burst out its back. Then it was on him.

But it didn't attack. Instead, it just grabbed Ashley as it ran over him, slamming a knee into his face. Shadow felt Ashley's fingers lose their grip as the incredibly strong wendigo picked her up without breaking stride.

Shadow ended up flat on his back, pain in his nose and warm blood covering his mouth and chin. He'd lost the gun. Scrambling to all fours, he felt around until he found the Sig Sauer. Once he had it, he looked after the wendigo, but could barely make anything out through the tears in his eyes. He wiped his face with a sleeve, but by then it was too late. Once the creature had taken Ashley, it had immediately gone off-road and into the nearby woods. He could see occasional flashes of it as it crashed through the brush, but couldn't get a clear view and couldn't risk a Hail Mary shot for fear of hitting his daughter.

Cursing, he pushed himself off the roadway and took off after the wendigo, but hadn't taken a dozen strides before he realized the thing was just too fast for him to catch. But he had an idea which way the wendigo would go, the same way it had gone when the other kids had been taken. Kentucky. It would go north. He skidded to a halt, turned and ran back toward the house.

CHAPTER TWENTY-EIGHT

"WHAT'S YOUR LOCATION, RANGER?"

Once inside, he grabbed his service belt, added a sheath knife to it, and put it on, jamming the Sig Sauer into its holster.. He wanted to be able to get to it in a hurry, after the fiasco out on the road. Glancing at the phone, he considered calling Jack, who, unlike Shadow, carried a cell phone, but decided it would take too much time. He picked up the new rifle, tore open a box of ammunition and loaded it. Then he chambered a round and put the safety on. Carrying the weapon and the snowshoes, still in their original carton, he fumbled his way out the door.

At the truck, he opened the passenger door and threw his stuff on the seat. He got in and started the engine. As soon as he started rolling, he grabbed the microphone from the clip on the dash.

"Breaks 23 to base."

"Go ahead, 23."

"We have a 10-65 in the park." That was the code for a missing person. Shadow had learned the codes a bit more than a year ago, and couldn't remember all of them, but was pretty sure there was no code for kidnapping and there sure as hell wasn't a code for kidnapping by monster. "My daughter's been abducted."

"Your daughter. . . What's your location, Fletcher?"

"She was taken just outside Rangers' Quarters. Perpetrator is heading northwest on foot. He'll probably cross the campground road and I'm on the way to intercept him."

"10-4, 23. I'll put out an alert. 4, did you copy?"

A male voice came from the speaker. "I copy. I'm rolling on it."

Bob Mathews was Breaks 4, Shadow knew. A good ranger, young and strong and devoted to his duties. Still, Shadow hoping to confront the wendigo first. He'd already learned that a round from a service pistol wouldn't stop the thing, but the .308 might at least slow it down. Maybe being immortal didn't mean it couldn't be killed, maybe it meant wendigos didn't die of old age. After all, wendigos came from a time before there were powerful rifles.

"Shit." He cried as he reached the end of the road and almost collided with a car turning in from the park road. It was Xan, coming for lunch. He hit the brakes and slid in the new snow, ending up facing back toward his house. Putting the transmission in reverse, he backed up onto the park road until he was facing north, then hit the gas.

In the rear-view, he saw that Xan had gotten out of her car and was standing in the road watching him leave. She had her hands on her hips, as though angry. That didn't matter at the moment. All that sliding around had wasted precious seconds.

The radio burst into life. "Breaks 8 to Breaks 12."

Jack! Shadow wanted to grab the microphone and reply, but The Claw wasn't up to that and he needed his left hand for steering on the slippery road. He reached the right hand turnoff for the campgrounds and slowed. No more slipping and losing control.

"Breaks 8 to Breaks 12."

Shadow ignored it as he made the turn and then gunned it. Large, flat snowflakes began to fall and he could tell the wind was picking up, too. He was driving through a foot or more of snow that had fallen earlier, since this road wasn't used or cleared during winter. The road wound around—there were no straight roads in the mountains—forcing him to keep his speed down. He couldn't see the surface of the road, but could feel the rough ground if he got off course and pretty much stay on the asphalt. At least there was no danger of running into oncoming traffic. The campgrounds were entirely empty.

Just as he entered the first campground, C, he caught sight of the Wendigo, carrying a limp, lifeless Ashley. It came from the trees his right and would pass directly in front of him as it crossed the road. For a moment, he considered gunning the truck and running the son of a bitch over, but he'd be putting Ashley's life in danger—if she was still alive. He had to believe she was. He hit the brakes and came to a sliding stop. Grabbing the rifle, he threw the door open and flung himself out.

He ran at an angle that might intercept the wendigo before it could get by him and into the trees. He cursed the delay that had slowed him. As he drew close, it was obvious that he would fall short by several feet since the snow hindered him more than the powerful wendigo. It was going to get by and it was too fast to catch from behind.

In desperation, he swung the rifle sidearm and threw it into the wendigo's legs. It went down in a heap, Ashley falling into the snow a couple of feet away.

Shadow pulled the Sig Sauer from its holster with his right—and only—hand, knowing there was a round left in the chamber from his last encounter with the creature. He clicked the safety off. It was ready to fire.

The wendigo bounded back to his feet and Shadow came to a stop. He had a clear shot. He tried to slow his breathing as he pointed the Sig Sauer, aiming for the thing's head. A harder shot, but perhaps a head-shot would take it down. He released the safety. Dimly, he realized Ashley was screaming again. The smell of rotten flesh invaded his nostrils.

The wendigo dropped into a crouch as he fired and the shot missed. As Shadow took aim for a second shot, the creature picked up Shadow's rifle by the barrel and flung it. Shadow let off another round as he tried to duck, but the weapon hit his shoulder, knocking him off balance. He fell onto his back.

As he rolled over and struggled to get up, he was aware of the wendigo effortlessly lifting Ashley and starting off again. On his knees, he looked around for his pistol, but it must have fallen into the snow. The rifle's butt stuck out of the snow, though, so he picked it up instead.

The wendigo was on the move again, heading toward the nearby woods. Kneeling, he leveled the .308 and clicked the safety off. He knew he was taking a chance, especially now that he was forced to shoot right-handed. He'd practiced shooting a few times since losing his hand, but he wasn't as good a shot as before. But if the wendigo got into the trees, Ashley would suffer a horrible fate.

He aimed for the creature's leg. It was a moving target but it wasn't very far away. Shadow took a breath and squeezed the trigger. The high-powered bullet hit the wendigo in the right leg, just below the knee. Dead flesh exploded from its calf, taking half the meat off the bone. It cried out, but it wasn't a cry of pain. The thing was outraged. It didn't go down but now it was limping badly. The smell of gunsmoke filled Shadow's nostrils.

He grinned and lined up the sights for a second shot. Even if the wendigo was immortal, the shot had proved it could be wounded. Enough shots in the right places might cripple it.

He aimed carefully at the wendigo's other leg, took a breath and again squeezed the trigger. Nothing happened. The trigger had not reset after the first shot, as it should on an automatic weapon. Suddenly he realized that it hadn't ejected the shell casing from the fired round, either. It must have been damaged when it was being thrown around like a boomerang.

The wendigo was nearing the tree line, slowed down, but still moving much faster than Shadow would be able do with the snow hindering him. He tossed it aside and dug in the snow, searching for the Sig Sauer.

He found it after a few seconds but when he looked up, the creature and Ashley were gone into the woods.

John Bushore

CHAPTER TWENTY-NINE

WAS IT SYMPATHY

Shadow brushed snow off the cold steel of the automatic pistol, then returned it to his holster. Stumbling through the deep snow, he ran back to the truck.

He grabbed the package from the truck, ripped it open, and got out the snowshoes. Fumbling he strapped them onto his feet, tugged the knots tight. He awkwardly got to his feet, the wide stance forced by the snowshoes feeling totally foreign. When he turned to leave, one snowshoe came down on the other and he nearly fell but steadied himself on the door frame.

He set out briskly, confident he'd be able to catch the injured wendigo. Five steps later he fell. Feeling like he wore clown shoes on his feet, he managed to get back up, but fell again before he'd gone very far. As he struggled to his feet again, he realized he'd better give himself a crash course on snowshoe walking.

He remembered a video he'd watched online when shopping for the snowshoes. This time, instead of trying to walk, he slid each foot forward without lifting it very far, as though he were ice-skating and walking at the same time.

He angled over to where he and the wendigo had just fought. Once there, he picked up the broken rifle. It might not fire, but it was still useful. He held the muzzle in his right hand and started off again, using the .308 for balance, like a cross between a cane and a ski pole. It wasn't much help, but it was better than nothing.

The wind was getting stronger and the snowflakes weren't falling, but whirling through the air like a cloud of small moths.

The Wendigo's barefoot trail wasn't hard to follow; even a child could have done it. Shadow found himself looking for blood, as if tracking a wounded deer, but soon realized there would be no blood spoor. The wendigo didn't bleed.

The trail led northwest, toward Grassy Creek. Once they hit the edge of the Park's plateau, there were several trails the wendigo could use to descend the mountain.

He concentrated on improving his snowshoeing. It wasn't hard to get into a rhythm, but he had to keep his mind on it. Soon he was traveling almost as fast as he could have walked on clear ground. Soon he could walk without the aid of the rifle and he tossed it aside.

Turns were a bit of a bother, but the wendigo kept a straight course unless it was forced to veer around an obstacle. As long as he took the turns slow, however, Shadow managed to stay upright.

He thought about how the rifle shot had damaged the creature. Native American lore said the wendigo was immortal, and Shadow believed in the power of Indian spell, but those legends had originated hundreds of years ago, before firearms had come on the scene. He might not be able to kill it, but what about blowing it to bits, piece-by-piece? If you could hit it in the shoulder and blow its arm off, it would surely continue to fight, but it wouldn't be as powerful, would it? What if you could blow its head off? Shoot its eyes out?

Suddenly he broke out of the woods and he was lost in a world of strong wind and swirling snow and dense fog. He knew there were mountains off in the distance, but there was no sign of them. The park was so high he was inside the storm's cloud. He wasn't sure if this would be classified as a blizzard, but it was snowing harder than he'd ever seen in his life. Visibility was limited to a few yards. He couldn't see more than a few feet, which was troubling because the edge of the plateau was so near.

The trail abruptly turned left, so Shadow dutifully shuffled his snowshoes around until he'd lined up, then set forward again. The going seemed to easier, for some reason, but then he saw a colored marker on a nearby tree and knew now that he was on the Grassy Creek Overlook trail, which followed the edge of the plateau, affording hikers a spectacular view of the canyon below and the mountains beyond.

If the wendigo stayed on this trail, they'd cross the Laurel Branch, a small streambed that drained rainwater and snowmelt from the plateau into Grassy Creek. It would be dry this time of year. The path would turn south, running next to the streambed, and end up at the circular vehicle roadway, labeled as "Nature Drive" on the park's tourist brochures. From there the wendigo could take the Grassy Creek Trail or cut over to the Ridge Trail, which would meet up with the River Trail. Either way, he was going to head down the mountain.

The barefoot tracks were clear and distinct, so Shadow knew he wasn't far behind. It this weather, those prints would be filled with drifting snow within minutes. If he hadn't maimed the wendigo, he would probably be too far behind to continue the track. Was it just wishful thinking, or did the tracks show the wendigo limping more?

To Shadow's surprise, when the tracks reached the Laurel Branch, they turned south, following the trail. It would have been quicker to cross the stream and reach the Grassy Creek Trail, but it would have been harder going. Crippled and carrying a load, the creature had taken the easier route. If it continued on the trail, it would come out on the overlook near both the Grassy Creek trails.

Shadow didn't hesitate. He left the trail and set off. All he had to do was go a short distance downslope, cross the streambed and climb the rise on the other side. He'd be on the Grassy Creek trail, and would have gained a lot of ground.

But he hadn't considered trying to walk in the snowshoes on a slope while gravity pulled him forward. He was soon racing down the slope, trying to keep the snowshoes from entanglement. If possible, he would have fallen on his backside to stop his plunge, but his momentum wouldn't allow it. Somehow, he managed to keep his feet until he reached the narrow streambed. He stooped and tightened a snowshoe strap that had worked its way loose, then went on.

By the time he came out on new trail, he was winded. He ignored his exhaustion, however, and headed up. The slope was easier here, so he began to recover.

If the wendigo decided to take the Grassy Creek Trail, it would meet up face-to-face with Shadow. He considered waiting in ambush but couldn't risk the possibility of the creature taking another route.

Without warning, he came to a sharp rise. Flat stones had been set into the hillside to form a crude stairway. Mounting the steps sideways because of the snowshoes, he came out on a concrete pad—the overlook constructed for tourists to take photos of the canyon from behind a low brick wall. The overlook had been built atop a promontory with a sheer cliff that dropped straight down for hundreds of feet. On the side opposite the wall was a slight incline leading up to the road.

He scanned the snow-covered overlook for tracks, then walked up the slope to the road and looked around. The roadway had recently been plowed and very little snow was on the asphalt, but tracks would still show. And there were no tracks. The wendigo must have taken another route. His gamble of going off-trail had backfired.

Then the wind carried the faint smell of the wendigo's stench to Shadow. It came from his left, just below the overlook. The wendigo must be coming up the other side. This overlook was the junction for both trails.

Shadow quickly shuffled down and crouched beside the wall. He reached down with his good hand and undid the snowshoe fastenings. He pulled the Sig Sauer from its holster and waited, trying not to breathe loud enough to give him away.

The first thing he saw was Ashley, slung over the wendigo's shoulder on the side facing Shadow. It was a stroke of luck. He watched the Wendigo emerge onto the platform. In moments, it was walking right by him, ten feet away, unaware of danger. Ashley's head was down, so she hadn't noticed Shadow either.

Shadow didn't hesitate. He used the same tactic he'd used before, aiming low so Ashley couldn't be hurt. He aimed carefully at the knee of the creature's uninjured leg and pulled the trigger.

The sound of the shot echoed off the brick wall into his ears and the creature's stench was momentarily masked by the smell of gunsmoke. Shadow was close enough to see the bullet pass straight though the wendigo's flesh, just above the knee. All it left was a hole; the pistol didn't pack nearly the power of the .308 bullet that had done so much damage earlier.

The thing roared its anger and dropped Ashley like a sack of potatoes. Shadow winced, but the snow would probably break her fall.

Now there was no time to think as the creature turned to glare at him. It started forward, incredibly fast. Shadow leaped to his feet and aimed directly at the creature's face. His first shot took its left ear off. The second shot went right through its forehead.

It was on him. It slapped the gun from his hand and reached for his throat. Shadow ducked backward, and the motion caused him to slip on the snow-covered concrete. He went down, his back against the brick wall. Without hesitation, he lashed out with a boot and slammed it into the wendigo's knee, the one he'd just shot. His attacker came down next to him and he rolled away. He could hear Ashley screaming.

"Run," he cried. "Ashley, get away from here."

Shadow and the wendigo got to their feet, three feet apart. He assumed a wrestling pose, his feet poised for motion and wondered if there was some kind of wild wrestling move he could make. Not likely, having only one hand. Shit, maybe he should have studied kung fu or karate or something. Without a gun, he was nearly powerless. That thought reminded him of his sheath knife and he whipped it out with his good right hand. He'd do as much damage as he could, try to delay it long enough for Ashley to get a head start.

This was the first time Shadow had a chance to look at the thing's face. The most striking feature was something that wasn't there—its nose, perhaps lost to frostbite when the creature had still been human. It was bald and the skin was wrinkled and leathery, shrunken to highlight the skull beneath. Its lips had pulled back with the shrinking, also, exposing dirty, rotten teeth and nasty, scabrous gums. The eyes no longer looked human, dull, lifeless pupils dilated as though they had seen the brilliant light of sun on snow for far too long.

As before, he was naked, and Shadow could see he had a shrunken, floppy penis and withered scrotum.

A man would have focused his eyes on the knife, but the wendigo ignored it. Its long, bony arm flashed out toward Shadow's throat, the skeletal fingers held wide.

The thing was fast. He barely got The Claw up to block it, planning to strike with the knife if the opportunity arose. The wendigo grabbed hold of The Claw and jerked it, trying to pull Shadow to him.

And nearly fell on its backside as The Claw's straps were ripped off Shadow's arm. It recovered and stared at the apparently human hand in its grasp. Shadow took that moment of uncertainty to step forward and bury the knife in its chest.

With a roar, the wendigo dropped The Claw and slammed him into the wall as though he were a rag doll. Before he could even begin to rise, the creature was on him. It pinned him to the ground and wrapped both hands around his throat.

Shadow, who had already had the wind knocked out of him by the wall, felt like his windpipe was being crushed. He grabbed those ice-cold, bony arms in his hands and tried to pull them away, but it was no use. The wendigo wasn't using the stringy muscles in those emaciated arms; its strength came from a supernatural power.

Shadow could feel himself slipping away. His vision blacked out. He was loosening his grip on the arms when he heard strange, distant sounds, a roaring noise, followed by a screeching sound. Then came a sound so distinct that, even in his fuzzy state, he couldn't help but recognize—a gunshot.

The constriction around his throat went away and the weight on his chest disappeared. He gasped for air, still unable to see or move. He heard another gunshot and the wendigo's roar. Things slamming together and a curse in a familiar voice—Shawnee Jack's voice.

His brain clearing, he turned his head. Although his vision was blurred, he could see two humanoid shapes struggling beside a large, yellow, boxy object—Jack's Jeep. One of the shapes had the other by the hair and was slamming its head into the yellow object repeatedly. As his eyes focused, he could see that the Wendigo was the one doing the slamming. There was something odd about its head.

Jack needed help. He rolled over and began to crawl around in the snow. His pistol was somewhere near here.

The slamming noise stopped. He looked over. Jack was nowhere to be seen and the wendigo was coming back to finish him off. He struggled halfway to his feet and then the creature was on him again. It slammed him down on his back, at the base of the wall. It got atop him, pinning his right hand, and went for the throat again to finish him off. Shadow reacted instinctively with what had formerly been his dominant hand and tried to block his throat with the stub.

The wendigo batted the appendage away and got its fingers around him again. But not before Shadow had taken a deep breath. He might be about to die, but he wasn't going without a fight. He had the odd thought that at least he couldn't smell the creature, since he wasn't breathing. Everything seemed surreal, especially since a big chunk of the wendigo's skull was missing, apparently been shot away by Jack's .308.

Then someone came into his peripheral vision. It was Ashley. She hadn't run away like he asked, and had come right up to the wendigo as it choked him. *Damn that girl, why hadn't she run when he'd told her. Now he'd die in vain.*

Sobbing, Ashley dropped to her knees in the snow next to the two struggling opponents. She reached out a hand and gently touched the wendigo's elbow.

"Please," Ashley said. "Please don't kill my daddy."

Shadow was looking directly into the wendigo's face and was amazed to see some sort of emotion flicker across. Was it sympathy? Confusion? Or was it simply delight that the girl was still going to be dinner? In any case, its fingers loosened slightly.

Shadow didn't hesitate. He arched his body beneath the creature and freed his good hand. He didn't remove it, though; he grabbed the wendigo where it would still have some sense of pain if any human qualities endured—its ball sack. It roared in anger, but its fingers loosened even further. Shadow put his stump on the thing's chest and pushed upward as hard as he could, while bringing his other arm up and toward him. For all its strength, the wendigo was amazingly light.

Shadow launched it over the wall and out into the void.

He couldn't speak, but he thought, "Will a fall kill an immortal monster?

And he prayed that it would.

CHAPTER THIRTY

"WHY IS YOUR FACE ALL BLUE?"

Ashley threw herself down onto Shadow's chest, blubbering. She made it harder for him to catch up on his breathing, but he didn't mind. At least he was breathing again. The air coming into his body was cold and deliciously fresh and the snow that he lay in was cool and soothing. After a bit, Ashley quit sobbing and just sniffled once in a while. He could easily have taken a nap, except for that annoying siren, which was growing louder.

The siren grew close and then ceased. There came the sound of tires swishing through snow, car doors and voices.

"It's Shawnee Jack," said a woman's voice. Ranger McCoy, no doubt.

"Who?" Chief Ranger Martin's voice.

"Ranger Goodluck. His head is all bloody. He's dead."

"What in the hell is that awful smell?" Martin asked.

"Don't know, Chief."

"Who's that over by the wall?"

"Don't know, Chief."

"Well, go take a look. I'm calling this in."

The sound of footsteps and then Karen McCoy's face stared down at him.

"Shadder! Well, I'll be blankety-blank hornswoggled. What happened to you?"

"It's a long story, Karen."

"I'll bet. What did you fellers get into anyhoo? A grizzly bear?"

"Something like that." He felt his mouth twisting into a grin.

"Well, it must have been a grizzly or else the devil hisself. I never thought I'd see Shawnee Jack whipsawed."

Fear struck him. "Is he dead?"

"He looks to be." McCoy sighed. "The chief is calling the rescue squad, but it's for you. Why the hell is your face all blue?"

161

"No idea."

"Yer eyes are all bloodshot, too. I hear you done went and called in a 10-65. This your daughter?"

"Yes."

"Well, where in tarnation is the perp? He get away?"

"Far away."

"Can you give me a deescription?" she asked.

Shadow was having trouble getting his breath. "Not right now." He could hear a faraway siren coming up the mountain.

"Tarnation, Shadder. You been jabberin' all this time and you ain't told me. . ."

Chief Martin's face appeared in Shadow's field of vision.

"Fletcher, that you?"

Shadow didn't bother to answer. He closed his eyes, feigning unconsciousness.

*

The next morning, Shadow awoke to a vision of beauty. The nurse from before, Maddy Something-or-other, stood beside his bead, her fingers on his wrist and her eyes on a watch. She must have sensed him coming around, because she turned with a smile.

"Hello, astronaut."

He could feel himself grinning.

"Can you talk?" she asked.

"Uh. . .uh. . .I think so." His throat felt tight, but it didn't hurt to speak.

"Do you need a drink of water or something?"

He nodded his head. She took a container of water from the bedside stand and held it so he could sip from a straw.

"There are a bunch of cops outside," Maddy said, "and they want to talk to you really bad. The doctor said it would be okay, if you feel up to it."

Might as well get it over with. He let go of the straw and sank back into the bed behind him. "Sure, that would be fine."

She put the water down, then wrote something on a chart at the foot of the bed. "I'll let them in."

Sergeant Bednarski and Agent Langley soon came in. Chief Ranger Martin was with them, of course. There was barely enough room for the group to put chairs around his bedside.

After the pleasantries—along with a few glaring looks from Bednarski—Langley took out a small device.

"Would you mind if I recorded this session, Ranger?"

Shadow shook his head. "Go right ahead."

"Your daughter said you threw the kidnapper off the overlook. Is that right, Fletcher?"

Shadow nodded.

162

"So he's dead?"

"I would imagine so."

"Why did she say it was a monster?"

Shadow shrugged. "She's a kid. And he did look like a monster, somewhat."

"In what way?"

Choosing his words carefully, Shadow replied. "He was a big guy, but I think he was on drugs because he was skinny as a crack addict. He sure seems like he was high on something, because he was strong as hell. He was bald and had a face not even a mother could love. Not to mention that he stunk to high heaven."

Bednarski broke in. "What color were his eyes?"

"Brown," Shadow said, shifting his gaze to the cop. "But I don't think you'll be needing to put out an APB on him. He's right down there in the canyon, waiting for you."

"Waiting, yes," said Martin, "but his body is going to be hard to find. It snowed all night, so he's probably covered in a foot or more of snow."

Shadow had to fight breaking out in a grin. That was exactly how he had it figured. If there was a body to find. Was the wendigo truly immortal? Had it walked away from the fall.? And even if there was a body at the bottom of the canyon, it might be washed away in the floods that were sure to come with the melting of all that snow.

"So tell me exactly what happened yesterday, Fletcher. From the beginning, when your daughter was taken."

"Well, my daughter and I were taking a walk just outside rangers' quarters when some lunatic jumped out of the trees, knocked me over and picked up my daughter and ran back into the trees. I took a shot at him, but missed. But I figured he would have to go through the campground to get away with her, so I drove to the campground to intercept him, calling headquarters on the way. Then I. . ."

The way he told it, he'd taken another couple of shots but missed, then given chase in snowshoes. The snow would hide any tracks that might show otherwise. The only parts of the chase he'd have to be careful of was the beginning and the end, when Ashley had been a witness who might contradict him about the kidnapper being a monster. And who would believe a kid, sure to be hysterical when being kidnapped.

The scene of the fight wouldn't yield any evidence either. Many park rangers had trampled over the snow, obliterating any barefoot track. If they found any pieces of shot-away wendigo flesh, they'd have human DNA, no doubt.

No, he didn't want things to turn out the way they had at False Cape State Park last year. He'd made a fool of himself, telling the Chief Warden about his supernatural "feelings." This time, he'd kept his mouth shut.

*

When the three men had left, Nurse Maddy breezed in with a big smile.

"That wasn't so bad, now was it, Mr. Astronaut."

He grinned right back at her. "Oh, didn't I tell you? I flunked out and never became an astronaut. So they looked around for a place I couldn't screw up too much, and made me a park ranger."

"Let's get a full set of vitals, now." She picked up his hand and put her other hand to his wrist. When she was done, she took something from her pocket and looked him in the eye.

"Well, I can't say I'm glad to see you, considering the circumstances, but at least you're in better shape than last time. Who were you fighting this time?"

"Somebody a whole lot meaner that Boiler Ben," he replied.

"And here it is Christmas Day and all. Merry Christmas, Ranger, you're lucky to be alive." She smiled again. "Here."

She put a thermometer thingie in front of him, the kind that beeps when it's gotten its reading. He took it into his mouth.

She took a blood-pressure cuff from around her neck, the old fashioned type, with a squeeze bulb. She tightened it and then took off the stethoscope that she also wore around her neck. When she'd gotten her reading, she took off the cuff, but she didn't just rip off the Velcro. She used both hands and he enjoyed her gentle touch.

The thermometer beeped and she glanced at the readout, then shot the plastic probe cover into a nearby trash can.

"Now let's have a look at you."

She leaned over in front of him and gently lifted his hospital gown near his neck. He had a clear view of her cleavage, which seemed to pull his gaze down and down.

"Not bad."

She repeated the process on the other side. Did she always leave the two top buttons of her blouse undone? He hoped so; it would make for a more pleasant hospital stay. But she hadn't worn her buttons open on his previous hospital stay.

"Okay, now look straight at me," she said.

She stared into his eyes from only a few inches away. He'd never been this close to a girl before and not kissed her.

"A little bit of subconjunctival hemorrhaging—red eye—but not as much as I'd expect from someone who's been choked. Has anyone ever told you that your pupils have a very unusual shade of blue—sort of like river water? I noticed it the last time I took care of you."

Shadow could hardly get his tongue to move. "Uh, yeah. I guess. Maybe it's just because people don't expect blue eyes on an Indian."

She moved away, but not hurriedly.

"The doctor will be coming in shortly. Once he's done, we can see about letting your visitors in to see you. Your wife and daughter?"

"My daughter. The lady is a. . .friend." Did Nurse Maddy smile slightly when he'd said that? Then he had a sudden sinking feeling. "Unless it's Ranger McCoy—but you'd know *her* wouldn't you?"

Maddy wrinkled her nose. "Yeah, I'd know her." Then she smile brightly. "Say, I just had a thought. When they let you out of here and you're feeling okay, maybe I could come up to the top of the park and you could show me around."

It surprised him. "You've lived around here all your life and never been up to the park?"

"It's just another mountain." She shrugged. "Never had a reason to go up there—until now."

After she'd gone, Shadow wondered if Grandma Min had put another spell on him. He wouldn't put anything past that old girl.

John Bushore

www.ingramcontent.com/pod-product-compliance
Lightning Source LLC
Chambersburg PA
CBHW070924130626
46555CB00001B/268